"James!" Cady yelled. "There's a—"

Her cry was cut off by a piercing scream.

Bolt started. It was all James could do to grab the reins with one hand and wheel the horse around.

James's heart raced as he turned to see what had made the terrifying cry. . . . Above him, not ten feet away, a snarling panther crouched on a rocky ledge.

James fumbled for the rifle, then realized it had fallen off his lap when he'd spun around.

He glanced back at Cady. She was frozen in her tracks just twenty feet away.

"Run, Cady!" he shouted. "Run!"

The hairs on the back of his neck stood on end as the panther growled lowly.

"*Now!*"

Cady met his eye and held it for an instant. She winked coolly.

Then she darted for the gun.

Don't miss the other two books in this exciting western trilogy:

Across the Wild River

Along the Dangerous Trail

from HarperPaperbacks!

OVER THE RUGGED MOUNTAIN

BILL GUTMAN

HarperPaperbacks

A Division of HarperCollins*Publishers*

This is a work of fiction. The characters, incidents, and dialogues are products of the author's imagination and are not to be construed as real. Any resemblance to actual events or persons, living or dead, is entirely coincidental.

HarperPaperbacks *A Division of* HarperCollins*Publishers*
10 East 53rd Street, New York, N.Y. 10022

Produced by Daniel Weiss Associates, Inc., 33 West 17th Street, New York, New York 10011.

First printing: January, 1994

Printed in the United States of America

HarperPaperbacks and colophon are trademarks of HarperCollins*Publishers*

10 9 8 7 6 5 4 3 2 1

OVER THE RUGGED MOUNTAIN

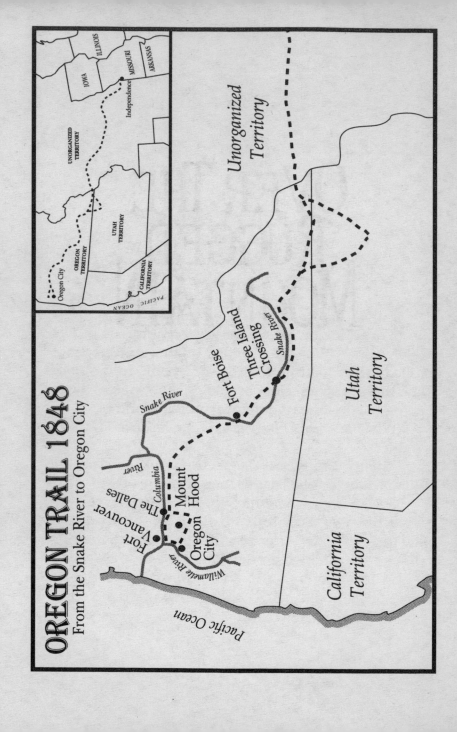

OREGON TRAIL 1848
From the Snake River to Oregon City

ONE

THE FIRST CONTEST

J ames Gregg sat in the tall grass of a high ridge overlooking the Snake River. Hundreds of feet below him, the wagons of the Stewart train rolled down the trail to the sandy bank. In the river lay three islands side by side. The wagons were going to cross the river by way of the islands.

"What a sight," James said to his friend Cady Walker.

"Mighty pretty," she agreed. "Look at how the ruts pick up on the islands, one after the other."

Not far from where the wheel ruts of the trail entered the river, they took up again on the nearest of the three islands. After crossing that island, the ruts dipped into the water, then emerged on the second island. And so on across the third and onto the far bank of the Snake, where they curled off to the north and west.

1

James and his family were traveling the Oregon Trail. It had been four months since they'd left Independence, Missouri, at the start of the trip. For almost a week, and over a hundred miles, they had hugged the south bank of the Snake River. Here at Three Island Crossing, they would ford to the north side and camp for the night.

"No wonder we didn't cross it before now," James said. "There's no other place as easy for fording."

"Oh, it still won't be *easy*," Cady assured him. "No fording ever is."

"You should know," James teased. At the beginning of the journey, Cady had fallen into the South Platte River during a fording.

"Humph," Cady said tartly. She didn't like to be reminded of how she'd almost drowned. Even less, of how James had saved her. "We best be getting along. They'll leave us behind if we're not careful."

"I reckon you're right." James stood and stretched. His body was stiff and sore from walking, but he hardly noticed it. He'd been sore for months.

"Race you to the bank," Cady said, getting up.

"Race me?" James guffawed. "Why, I can run *backward* faster than—"

Before he could finish, Cady was off. She ran down the left wheel rut, her long calico dress flapping behind her.

In a flash James was in the right rut. He clamped

his hat to his head with one hand and pumped with the other. Soon he was matching her stride for stride.

"See you yonder, tortoise girl!" he hollered.

Cady looked over at him and laughed. "Tortoise girl? Watch this, snail boy!"

Then, to James's amazement, she put her head down and commenced running in earnest. She pulled ahead of him, five feet, now ten.

James yanked his hat off his head and pumped hard with both arms. With each step, though, she increased the distance between them.

They were flying down the trail now. James could hear his heart pounding and the wind whistling in his ears.

Cady was tall and lanky, all bone and muscle. Still, James was surprised a girl could run so fast. But he figured he had better staying power than she did. If he could keep close, he'd beat her at the end.

Near the bottom of the slope was the wagon bringing up the rear of the train. Before she got to it, Cady jumped to the left, out of the wheel rut, to go around.

Seconds later, James leaped to the right.

"Go, Cady!" he heard someone in the train yell. "Don't let him catch you!"

"Get 'er, Jamie!" he heard someone else, maybe his brother Jeremy, shout. "Get 'er!"

Folks all up and down the train urged one or the other of them. As best as he could tell, he and Cady were getting equal encouragement.

James's throat burned; his head throbbed. He was gasping for breath. He felt as if he were running through molasses. Even his hat felt heavy in his hand.

Cady was still going strong.

Why had he agreed to this silly race, anyway? Who'd be crazy enough to want to run after a whole long day of walking?

Cady glanced over her shoulder, met his eye, and cackled loudly.

James put his head down and did his best to make his worn-out legs move faster.

Now she was at the head of the train, darting past Colonel Stewart, the train boss, and Pierre Delaroux, the guide.

Go, go, go! James screamed to himself. He'd figured Cady would tire at the end. But if anything, she was running faster now than she had been at the start.

It was no use, he realized. His legs were like taffy. He'd never catch her.

Cady was only a hundred yards from the bank of the Snake, and James still trailed her by a good thirty or forty feet.

She hopped nimbly back into the left rut. Then, when James was about to jump into the right rut, he saw Cady stumble. To James's astonishment and

4

glee, she went flying, spread-eagle on her belly, her face in the dust.

Here was his chance. Deciding not to run in the rut, James put on an extra burst of speed, every muscle in his body burning.

Cady was on her feet again in seconds, but by then James was past her.

He was almost there. If he could only make it before collapsing in exhaustion . . .

Thirty more feet, twenty, ten, and finally he stopped at the edge of the river, chest heaving.

He fell over sideways and rolled onto his back, letting his shoulders sink into the cool wet sand of the bank.

A moment later Cady flopped down beside him.

"You lose," James gasped. "Tortoise girl."

"I had you beat," Cady replied between breaths. "Till I tripped on the hem of my dress."

"You didn't trip over your dress," James said, eyes closed. "You were trying to show off by running in the rut. I won fair and square."

Cady dug a fistful of wet sand and slapped it onto James's chest. "I'll beat you next time. You'll see."

"Sore loser," James muttered, scraping the sand off his shirt.

TWO

THREE ISLAND CROSSING

"Jamie, I'm surprised at you," Jeremy said. "Almost letting a girl beat you like that."

James glanced at his older brother. They were huddled in the wagon with their six-year-old sister, Elizabeth, and James's dog, Scraps. The wagon was bobbing in the Snake River now, halfway between the southern bank and the first island.

Ma and Pa rode on the front board, steering the oxen. James's horse Bolt, along with their other horses, Corncob and Mackle, waded through the chest-high water. The wagon bumped and swayed gently in the current.

"I was just being polite," James said. "Something you'd know nothing about."

"If you were just being polite," Elizabeth asked innocently, "why didn't you let Cady win in the end?" She fixed her big blue eyes on James.

7

Jeremy snorted. "Good question, Elizabeth."

"It's polite to give a person a chance," James said loftily, "but it's ungentlemanly to lose on purpose. Even to a girl."

"Ungentlemanly, maybe. But beating her in a footrace is no way to win a girl's affections." Jeremy was fifteen. He liked to think of himself as an expert in affairs of the heart. "Why, I remember one time, Missy and I were—"

"I'm not trying to win her affections," James interrupted testily. "And if I have to listen to another story about the wonderful Miss Missy, I'll jump in the river and swim to Oregon City."

Missy was Jeremy's sweetheart back in Pennsylvania. For a long time Jeremy had been angry about having to leave her, and he'd hardly spoken to anyone.

But that had changed after he heard the rumors of gold. He couldn't stop talking about heading south to California and sending for Missy after he'd made his fortune.

Jeremy gave James a hurt look. "Suit yourself," he said.

Now James felt bad that he'd cut his brother off. He looked over at Jeremy, who was staring dejectedly out the back of the wagon. Just then the wagon's wheels hit the banks of the first island, and the wagon resumed its familiar overland rocking and jolting.

"All right." James rolled his eyes. "What were you going to tell me about Missy?"

"Well," Jeremy said, brightening. "It was one day last fall. Missy was looking particularly fetching in a blue gingham dress and pretty little sunbonnet. . . ."

James sighed. *Wake me when it's over,* he thought, and took to staring dejectedly out the back of the wagon himself.

By the time they reached the banks of the second island, Jeremy was finishing his story.

". . . And then we bade each other farewell, and promised to meet again the next day," he concluded.

"Goodness, that certainly was interesting," James said politely. He stifled a yawn. "Maybe I'll go see how the Walkers are doing." He scurried off the wagon before his brother could launch in on another Missy story.

When he arrived at the Walkers' wagon, James wasn't sure whether he should call out for Cady. She might be angry at him still, over the footrace. He walked alongside their wagon, trying to decide what to do.

Then Mr. Walker, who was up front driving the oxen, hollered, "Jamie, good to see you!"

James waved. Oh, well. Now Cady knew he was there. He'd have to talk to her, whether she was mad or not.

Cady popped her head out of the back of the

wagon. "Howdy, James." She smiled, and ducked back in.

He heard her ask her mother for permission to walk for a while. Mrs. Walker said yes.

Cady climbed out of the wagon and trotted up alongside James. He tipped his hat warily. "Cady," he said.

"James," she said in a deep voice, mocking him.

He stared straight ahead for a moment. "You're not angry?"

Cady laughed. "Why should I be angry? Just because I tripped on my dress in a silly old race?"

James eyed her suspiciously. "You seemed angry at the time." He picked up a stone and tossed it in the river.

"I got over it. Besides, I'll beat you next time. In whatever kind of contest." She threw a stone past where James's had landed.

James decided it was time to change the subject. "Lately your ma seems . . . I don't know. Softer, somehow. Less worried." He didn't want to say that she seemed a lot nicer, too. For a long time, Mrs. Walker had been jumpier than a cat in a thunderstorm.

"I know," Cady said. "I've been spending a lot more time with her. Like I used to."

"Used to?" James was surprised to hear that.

"Mother wasn't always so mean and horrible, you know."

"I don't think your mother's—"

"You don't have to lie, James," Cady said. "I know how you must hate her. It's a terrible thing to say, but I hated her myself at times. Always thumping on her Bible, reading those awful verses. But she wasn't like that before."

James waited for her to go on.

"Scott was sickly for years," she said quietly. "It drove Mother mad to watch him waste away."

"It was hard on all of you," James argued.

"Not like it was on Mother," Cady said. "Maybe you can't understand it, being a boy."

James was about to object, but Cady went on quickly. "I've been turning it over and over in my head, James. You see, Mother loved Scott with all her heart. More than Father or I did, even. More than anything in the world."

Cady squinted at the sky speculatively. "I reckon it was the scariest thing she could imagine—her own child dying. And it made her so afraid, she came to be frightened of everything—strangers, the land. Even me and Father. So she hid in the Bible, where she found words that backed up her fears. And when Scott died . . . well, the worst had happened. Her worst fear came true. And what could be scarier than your worst fear come true?"

"Nothing?" James guessed.

"Exactly," Cady agreed. "After your worst fear, anything else doesn't look scary at all. So her fears just went away." She picked up a stone and tossed it in her hand. "Scott is with the angels now, blessing us. That's what she believes. And I reckon I believe it myself."

Cady gave a little half smile. "As much as I miss him, maybe his death was a blessing from God. And you know, Mother has another blessing on the way."

James understood she was referring to the child her ma was carrying. Mrs. Walker had been looking goodly round for weeks. The baby would be due soon.

Cady hurled the stone way out into the river. "Now beat that, if you can."

On the third island James paid a visit to Will Gantry and his new bride, Sara. When Sara's parents, the Jenningtons, lost their wagon after it slid off the trail, they had been taken in by the Teagues. James found Will and Sara at the Teagues' wagon.

"Why, Jamie, isn't this delightful?" Sara asked. "Just smell that clean air, and look at this beautiful river all around us!"

James sniffed, and looked around. The river was awfully impressive. "Mighty pretty," he agreed. He liked how cheerful Sara was, even despite her injury. Her hip had been permanently damaged in the fall that destroyed her parents' wagon. Because she still couldn't walk much, she rode in the Teagues' wagon most of the time.

"It's pretty, all right," said Will. "But I hear the

country in California is the most beautiful of all."

James shot Will a dark look. He didn't like all this talk of California. Ever since Sara was injured, Will had been wanting to go to California and strike it rich. He thought gold could mend Sara's busted leg.

"They say Oregon's as nice as anyplace," James muttered.

"Oh, it is, it is," Will said. "Particularly for a farmer, like yourself. But California is where the gold is—where fortunes are made. I know my Sara would love to see that country. Wouldn't you, dear?"

"Of course." James could tell her smile was forced.

A troubled look crossed Will's face. "Well, I'd best saddle up Tempest," he said, a little too loudly. "I mean to ford the last section of river on horseback. Pierre Delaroux asked me to help him scout tonight's campsite." He clapped his hands. "I'd best be going."

"What got into him?" James wondered out loud as Will departed.

Sara's face was flushed—two bright red patches on her cheeks, and one on her forehead. "Oh, Jamie, can't you see how badly he wants to go to California?" she cried. "He must *hate* me for keeping him back!"

"Hate you?" James echoed, astonished. He knew what she was thinking—that Will didn't want to have to take care of a crippled wife. That Will resented the burden. "It's not true," he insisted.

Sara brushed at a thick lock of black hair that had fallen over her eyes. "He must hate me," she repeated.

James wanted to climb into the wagon and hold her, comfort her. But he knew he couldn't do a thing like that.

THREE

THE SECOND CONTEST

In his travels, James had seen herds of buffalo that blanketed the prairie to the horizon. Gopher towns that seemed to stretch on forever. A flock of passenger pigeons that took half an hour to fly overhead.

But nothing compared to the millions of jackrabbits on the north side of the Snake. The plain was swarming with them, their long ears flopping and scrawny legs stretching in the dust. The lead oxen almost had to step over them. And the moment the train passed, the trail was littered with rabbits again.

Game on the south side of the Snake had been scarce. The week before, Pa had received dried salmon roe in exchange for fishhooks from some Bannock Indians. But the last of the salty fish eggs was gone. For days the Greggs had eaten nothing

15

but the stores of grain and dried meat they'd brought with them.

Colonel Stewart had decided to spend the day camped on the north bank of the Snake. The emigrants needed a day of rest, and with all the rabbits, there would be good hunting.

James's mouth watered at the thought of roasted rabbit. He ran to the wagon to get his rifle. Pa and Jeremy were already gathering their guns.

"Take careful aim, boys," Pa said. "We don't want to be wasting any bullets."

"I'll aim," James said with a grin. "Though I could hardly miss if I tried, there are so many of them."

"Then let me take a crack at them," came a voice from behind him. It was Cady.

James turned. "You've never even shot a gun before." He waved a hand to dismiss her.

"So?" Cady replied. "I never rode a horse before this summer, and now I ride fine."

Cady had been practicing on Corncob, the Greggs' old mare.

"Shooting a gun's a little more dangerous than riding a horse," James assured her. Sometimes Cady acted so grown up, like when she was talking about her ma. Other times she was just childish. "You could hurt somebody if you're not careful. And I don't want you scaring off all the rabbits."

"I'll be careful," Cady said. "Besides, there are so many rabbits, a person would practically have to

16

miss on purpose. You said so yourself."

James scrunched up his face. "I didn't mean—"

"Jamie," Pa said. "Why don't you show Cady how to handle the rifle? She needs to know, now that we're out west."

"But Pa," James argued, "she can't even—"

"She can learn," Pa said mildly. "No time like the present. Now you two head off that way." He motioned to the right side of the train. "Jeremy and I will go toward the river."

James gave his pa a pained look.

"I bet we catch more than you do," Jeremy said, trying to make a game of it.

"We'll have no wagering around here," Pa said sternly. Then he smiled. "But let's say whichever team brings home the fewest rabbits has to clean everyone's dinner plates. For the next week."

That was a lot of plates. Cady and her parents always ate dinner with the Greggs. And many nights they were joined by the widow Loughery and Pierre Delaroux, or by Will and Sara Gantry. Sometimes even Sara's parents, the Jenningtons, and their friends the Teagues—all six of them—joined in the meal. On plenty of occasions more than a dozen people sat around the Greggs' nightly fire.

"No fair," said Cady. "You'll have two guns, and we have only the one. And I'm just a beginner. You should have to catch twice as many as we do."

"Or three times as many," James added sourly.

17

Pa and Jeremy exchanged looks.

"It's a deal," Pa said. "Three of ours for every one of yours. Dinner plates washed—and dried—by the losers."

"Good luck." Jeremy tipped his hat at Cady. Then he and Pa set out on the shoot.

James sighed and grabbed the rifle. "Let's get going," he grumbled. "We'll have to move fast if we don't want to wash their plates tonight."

The plain stretched out in all directions, merging on the shimmering horizon with the sky. Uncounted jackrabbits leaped and bounded over the earth, sending up small puffs of dust with each jump.

As they made their way across the plain, James gave Cady a lesson in how to use a rifle. First he showed her how to carry it safely—barrel over the shoulder.

"That way, the bullet won't dribble out," he explained. "And if it fires accidentally, no one will get hurt."

"Makes sense," Cady said, nodding.

Then he showed her how to clean the gun. He unhooked the long ramrod that was stored beneath the barrel. Fixing a small cloth to the end of it, he ran it down the barrel several times.

"When you get back to camp, you should clean your gun with boiling water and then oil it," James told Cady. "But out here in the wilderness, clearing the barrel has to suffice."

Next he poured powder into the barrel, wrapped a bullet in a small piece of oiled cloth, and slid them down. He carefully tamped the bullet with the ramrod. Finally he showed her how to fit the percussion cap under the cock.

"You have to go through all this every time you want to fire?" Cady asked.

"Yes, you do," James said seriously. "And if you don't do it right, *every time*, the gun could blow up in your face."

"Mercy on us." She shook her head. "I had no idea it was so complicated."

"You sure you want to go on with this shoot?" he asked. He was hoping she'd give up and let him go alone.

"You know I aim to take care of myself." Cady looked him in the eye. "Especially now."

James knew she meant now that Scott was gone.

"All right," James said. "Let's get us some rabbit."

The jackrabbits kept their distance. Dozens at a time would bound away in a wave when Cady and James got too close. After scampering a few yards, the rabbits would settle down again. Then the two hunters would once again approach—and the rabbits would flee in another wave.

"We should be as close to them as we can when

19

we fire," said James, loading the gun. "I'll go first. You watch."

James crawled in the dirt, Cady behind him. He had his eye on a gray-and-black one near a clump of sage. It wasn't fat—no jackrabbit ever was. But it was big, and James reckoned those stringy legs would make a right tasty stew.

He inched forward slowly. The rabbit eyed him warily.

James brought the gun up to his shoulder and peered down the barrel. The rabbit's nose twitched.

Crack!

The rabbit sprang several feet into the air, twisting jerkily. By the time it hit the ground, it was dead.

"That's one," James said matter-of-factly. "Pa and Jeremy need three now."

He scrambled to his feet, then turned to Cady. She was sitting in the dirt, her face pale, her hands clapped over her ears.

"That was *loud*." She took her hands off her head. "And it happened so quick. One minute he was a cute little rabbit—"

"And the next minute, he was rabbit stew," James finished for her. "You still fixing to shoot something? Or have you lost the stomach for it?"

Cady sneered at him. "Give me that rifle," she muttered, rising and snatching it out of his hands.

James tied the dead jackrabbit by the legs and slung it over his shoulder. The other rabbits had been frightened by the shot, so Cady and James had to walk nearly half a mile before catching up to them again.

Just as she'd seen James do, Cady loaded the gun, then crawled on her belly toward the rabbit she'd picked out. But before she had a chance to fire, her prey scampered away.

"What did I do wrong?" she asked in consternation.

"You tried to get too close." James smirked. "You have to have a feel for how near you can get. I reckon you just don't have it."

"I have it!" Cady snapped. "You watch."

Again she commenced crawling toward a rabbit. This time she was more cautious. The rabbit was a good fifty feet away when she raised the rifle.

James was about to tell her to go on, get closer, when he thought better of it. No, let her miss. That would teach her.

Crack!

James watched in satisfaction as the rabbit she'd been aiming at bounded away unharmed.

Cady lay on the ground, clutching her right shoulder. She was grimacing in pain.

"I feel like somebody ran up and whacked me in the shoulder with a fence post," she said through clenched teeth.

"I forgot to warn you," James said innocently. "A rifle like that gives quite a kick. You get used to it after a while. Oh, and nice shot," he added dryly.

21

"Shut up," she said grumpily. "And help me clean the barrel. I want another try."

James could see he'd better get used to cleaning. He'd be doing a lot of it in the next week.

At the end of the day, Cady and James brought only two rabbits back to the wagon.

Cady had kept insisting on another try. By the fourth shot, she was getting close enough to the target to have a chance. Even so, she kept missing. Finally her shoulder was so sore from the gun's kick that she couldn't bear to fire again.

James took the gun from her and, in the dying light, managed to shoot another rabbit.

Pa and Jeremy brought in five each.

Twelve rabbits wasn't bad for one day. Plus Mr. Walker, Cady's father, had shot four more himself.

James's ma and Mrs. Walker decided to cook five of them that night as a small feast. The other eleven would be hung from the rafters of the wagons to dry. The pelts would be tanned, then sewn into gloves, hats, and other small items. Mrs. Walker was planning on making some bunting for the baby on the way.

All around the nightly circle, the delicious smell of meat roasting rose into the air. Though the Teagues and Jenningtons had their own fire going, Will and Sara brought three rabbits over to the Greggs' fire and joined them for dinner. As did the widow Loughery and Pierre Delaroux.

After the last rabbit was picked clean, James licked the fat off his fingers. He sighed contentedly. He was stuffed.

Still, he wasn't completely happy. He knew he could have brought home five rabbits, as his brother and pa had, if Cady hadn't been hogging the rifle.

He looked at the tin plates stacked around the fire. "Time to get to work, Cady," he said grouchily. "And *you're* washing."

And so Cady, grimacing all the while from the pain in her shoulder, washed, while James dried.

Tomorrow, she insisted, they'd switch jobs.

FOUR

POACHED SALMON, WESTERN STYLE

The day after the rabbit shoot, the emigrants set out again. They were heading toward Fort Boise, on the banks of the Snake River, one hundred and fifty miles to the northwest.

The north side of the Snake River was flatter and less rocky than the south side. And because the emigrants would be cutting straight across the open plain to Fort Boise, rather than following the curve of the river, the northern route was two days quicker.

Before they reached the fort, however, Silas Moss, a man only a few years older than Will, died suddenly of a fever. He'd been traveling alone on the train, as an outrider. Over the months he'd attached himself to the Smoot family. The Smoots had already lost a little son, Jasper, so the death of Silas was doubly hard.

25

Silas had family back in Ohio, and Mr. Smoot took it upon himself to write them the sorrowful news. The letter would be mailed at the fort, taken through Canada to Montreal, and from there forwarded to the Mosses in Ohio.

Silas was buried in a barren rocky field, his grave marked only by a pile of stones.

After a long day of walking in deep wheel ruts, the emigrants halted near a hot springs. A group of Bannock Indians was camped nearby. James hoped these Bannocks were offering something a little more tasty than fish eggs.

He was relieved when Pa returned from his bartering with four small salmon, which the Indians had caught in a nearby stream. James liked salmon, even if he didn't care for their eggs.

"And I'll be cooking them a special way tonight, too," Pa said, cleaning the fish with his long sheath knife.

"*You'll* be doing the cooking tonight?" Ma laughed. "That's already special enough for me."

"Well, the children may want to help." Pa tossed the fish guts to Scraps, James's little dog, who set upon them greedily. "After I show them the special method the Indian fellows taught me."

"The Indians taught you how to cook?" Elizabeth asked.

"Why, sure, Elizabeth," Pa said. "They know lots of things we don't—all about the animals, and the plants, and the land. They have medicines most white folks have never even heard about, made from things like roots and bark. They even know how to cook up a hot meal right in the ground."

"In the ground?" James asked. "What do you mean by that?"

"You'll see," Pa assured him.

James had often admired the way the Indians were able to live off the land so skillfully. They survived in parts of the country the wagon trains moved through as quickly as possible. He was glad Pa admired them too.

Still, that last remark, about cooking in the ground, troubled James. He wondered if perhaps Ma shouldn't go ahead and make dinner, as she usually did.

Pa gathered up the cleaned fish and got out four long sticks, a big platter, and forks and plates for everyone. Then he commenced walking away from camp.

Now where was he going? James exchanged puzzled looks with Ma, Jeremy, and Elizabeth. They all set out after him.

Low, flattish mountains surrounded the basin of the Snake River. The way they rolled into the distance, one behind the other, reminded James of parts of Pennsylvania. Except back east the mountains were gently rounded. Here the mountains looked as if they'd had their tops shaved off.

After a half mile of walking, they arrived at the hot springs. Pa handed James, Jeremy, and Elizabeth sticks.

"One for each of my three good children," he said. Then he took a fish and speared it onto the remaining stick. "Watch this."

He went over to a shallow part of the hot springs and dipped the fish directly in the steaming water. "Tonight we're having poached salmon, western style."

Suddenly James lost his appetite. The water looked clear enough, and he supposed his pa knew what he was doing. Nevertheless, boiling food right in the earth wasn't James's idea of a treat.

He wondered how the fish would taste. Probably not as good as roasted over a fire, or fried, the way Ma cooked them. He didn't fancy eating something that tasted like dirt.

He looked at his brother and ma. Jeremy didn't look any more pleased about Pa's new cooking method than James was. Even Ma seemed unsure.

"Papa's cooking the fish in the ground!" Elizabeth exclaimed, laughing delightedly. "The Indians showed him how!"

There's a six-year-old for you, James said to himself. *If she was old enough to know better, she'd be troubled too.*

Not ten minutes later Pa withdrew the fish and placed it on the platter. He cut it open and passed around small chunks for his doubting family to sample.

James examined his morsel carefully. The pink flesh smelled pleasant enough. It even seemed to be cooked all the way through. He put it in his mouth and chewed.

It was tender and savory, with a slightly salty flavor. It didn't taste like mud at all. In fact, it was delicious.

James looked at his ma and at Jeremy. They looked as pleased with their bites as he was with his.

And so James hurried to spear his own fish and plunge it into the wondrous hot springs. He wanted to do as the Bannocks did and prepare poached salmon, western style.

FIVE

LORD CALLANBRIDGE

A week later the emigrants reached the Boise River. The Boise was also known as the Bigwood River, for the large balms and cottonwoods that grew on its shady banks.

After following the Boise for several days, and fording it once, the train rolled up to the gates of Fort Boise. The fort was a mile north of where the Boise River emptied into the Snake.

James was eager to explore another western outpost. Frontier settlements were gathering places for all manner of men and women. Indians looking to trade meat and pelts for guns and liquor camped outside the walls.

At Fort Laramie and Fort Hall, James had met trappers, cavalrymen, guides. No government ruled the forts, and the fur companies that operated them had only the loosest authority. In the West every man was free.

31

Knowing that Will would be as keen on visiting a new fort as himself, James ran to the Teagues' wagon. There he found Will preparing to set out. Slung over his shoulder were more than a dozen rabbit pelts.

"Guess you've been eating an awful lot of rabbit stew lately," James observed.

"That's right," Will said in his smooth Virginia drawl. "I've had about enough to last me a lifetime. Last night I tried to add up how many rabbits I shot before we reached the Boise. You want to know what it came to?"

"How many?"

"Thirty-seven. Give or take a couple. Plus Mr. Jenning—er, Father, shot nearly as many. And then Harlan Teague shot a couple dozen. We're so weighed down with rabbits, the oxen can barely pull the wagon!"

"What are you going to do with those boys?" James asked, indicating the pelts heaped on his back.

"I plan on bartering them at the fort. Care to come along?"

"Would I ever!" James grinned. "I was hoping you were headed that way."

They walked across the short stretch of dusty ground between the circle of wagons and the gates of the fort. Some Bannock Indians were camped just outside the fort. Their wickiups looked a lot like the tepees of the Plains Indians, except they were rounded at the top instead of pointy. Farther off were some other Indians who weren't Bannocks. James didn't know what they were called.

"What are you going to get for the rabbits?" James asked. "A knife, or a gun?"

"I was hoping to find a gift for Sara," Will answered.

"Like a blanket, maybe? I hear the winters are awfully cold and wet in Oregon City."

Will laughed. "A *blanket*? That's no gift fit for a young lady. Sara likes fineries."

"You think so?" James asked doubtfully. "You ever asked her?"

Will blinked. "I don't have to. I know how she feels. I'm going to trade for a nice pocket watch. As fancy a one as I can find."

"A fancy pocket watch!" James snorted. "Why, Sara doesn't need a pocket watch. A farmer's wife sets her time by the sun—you can ask my ma."

"Jamie, I know she doesn't *need* a watch." Will halted. "But I want to give her something pretty. And she's not going to be a farmer's wife. I'll be sending for her in California, soon as I strike it rich."

"Sara doesn't want to be rich," James said. Why couldn't his friend see the terrible mistake he was making? "She just wants to be happy."

"That's right!" Will shot back. "And I intend to get her something to make her happy, even if she doesn't need it."

"Will," James started, "you can't just—"

"I have to get her something," Will said. "I have to show her how much I love her."

"But—"

"You recall when we were walking on the island together?" Will asked. "Did you see the way she looked at the thought of going to California with me? She must hate me!"

"You're wrong," James insisted. "Sara loves you. She could never hate you."

"She does!" Will fairly shouted. "It was *my* fault she was hurt in the fall. I should have done something to protect her. And now I have to make it up to her—buy her everything she needs, and everything she *doesn't* need too." Will commenced walking quickly to the fort.

James sighed quietly to himself and stumbled miserably after his friend.

As they passed through the gates, a man on horseback galloped out of the fort. Behind him a second horse, loaded down with a number of large bags, was led by a rope. They nearly trampled Will and James in the narrow opening to the fort.

"Hey, watch where you're going!" James yelled after the man, who never looked back.

Fort Boise was a low, rectangular structure of timber and mud. Lining the inside of the wall were mean little rooms—some used as stalls for horses and cows, others as bunks for company agents. In the central yard traders hawked furs and meat. Indians offered blankets and moccasins. Smithies, wheelwrights, and barrel makers busied themselves. Soldiers in dirty blue uniforms filed by. Sheep and pigs hustled through the confusion.

Like forts Laramie and Hall, Fort Boise was filthy, smelly, dusty, crowded, loud, and shabby—and thoroughly fascinating to James.

"I'm sorry I shouted at you, Jamie," Will said over the racket. "I know you mean well. Please help me find someone who might be dealing in watches."

James nodded wretchedly.

For some minutes they scanned the yard for likely prospects.

Then James spotted a young man about Will's age dressed in a long black topcoat, gray pants with a thin green stripe down the sides, and glossy black shoes. On his head he wore a beaver-pelt top hat, and around his neck was wrapped a flowing bright red cravat. He had a ring on every finger of both hands and was holding a walking stick.

Now, strange dress was hardly unusual on the frontier. When clothing wore out, it was replaced by whatever was available. Trappers wrapped themselves in rudely sewn deerskin leggings. Soldiers draped buffalo cloaks Indian style over their shoulders, sometimes adding feathers to their hair to complete the effect. Antler points and coyote teeth served as clasps and buttons or were strung on strips of leather for show. James had seen a coonskin cap so rudimentary, it looked as if the raccoon hadn't ceased breathing.

Even so, this young dandy with the rings and the topcoat struck the eye.

"That fellow looks like the sort who might be carrying a fancy watch." James pointed out the man to Will.

"He certainly does," Will agreed. "Let's introduce ourselves."

They made their way through the crowded yard toward the dandy.

Will stepped up and extended his hand. "Will Gantry, at your service."

The man jumped like a startled jackrabbit. "Almaris Drummond Belvoir, the seventh Lord Callanbridge." He and Will shook hands.

Almaris *what*? James asked himself. This fellow seemed to talk kind of funny. And did he call himself a lord, as in dukes and duchesses?

"This is my friend James Gregg," Will said in a friendly tone.

Lord Callanbridge offered his hand, and James shook it. "Pleased to meet you, sir," James got out. He'd never shaken hands with a titled person before. He was careful not to squeeze the rings too tight.

"You don't look like you're from around here," Will observed casually.

James was impressed with the way Will acted so

natural. If Will hadn't been there, James probably would have got down on one knee and bowed or something. What did one do in the presence of nobility?

"Don't I?" said the lord. He seemed truly surprised. "Dear me. I shall have to remedy that upon my man's return."

James watched with interest as Lord Callanbridge dug in the inside pocket of his topcoat. He drew out a pair of folded spectacles, flattened them, and placed them carefully on his nose. Then he brought out a large gold pocket watch attached to a long chain.

James glanced at Will, whose eyes were locked on the watch.

"I say!" The lord was staring at the watch too. "Smithers left at half past with my traveling kit to check into the hotel. That was nearly an hour ago. Where can he be?"

"Who's Smithers?" Will asked.

"Why, my man," the lord explained. "Smithers is my hired man."

"And how long have you known him?"

"We met this morning." Lord Callanbridge beamed.

"Er, Lord—Cullenbridge, was it?" Will started.

"Almaris Drummond Belvoir," said the dandy. "Lord Callanbridge, to some. But you may call me Al. I do so enjoy these informal American manners."

Land's sakes! James said to himself. *A real lord, and he acts just like regular folks.*

"Well, Al," Will said, "I don't know how to tell you this, but there's no hotel here."

"No hotel?" Lord Callanbridge unclipped the spectacles from his nose. "Surely there must be. Smithers is securing a room for me as we speak."

"I'm afraid Mr. Smithers, if that's his name, is hightailing it for Fort McKenzie. Or some other place where he can sell your kit." Will shook his head. "We saw a man leaving with a loaded-down horse when we came in, didn't we, Jamie?"

James nodded quickly.

"You've seen the last of Smithers," Will concluded.

"But my clothing!" Lord Callanbridge exclaimed. "My collections!"

"Collections?" James asked.

"Why yes, my birds." Lord Callanbridge mopped his brow with a large white handkerchief. "I'm here on a scientific expedition, to carry on the work of the great Mr. Townesend. All my life I've read of the great American wilderness. The unnamed species, the exotic natives—no offense, I'm sure. And now here I am, experiencing it firsthand! Already I've cataloged two new buntings and three grackles."

"I'm afraid your grackles are gone," James pointed out politely. "And your buntings."

"Along with your clothes," Will added.

"Quite," the lord agreed.

Will and James exchanged looks. "Look here, friend," said Will. "Why don't you join us on the wagon train? We're heading for Oregon City. Once you're there, you can send word back to England for further supplies."

"I'm not sure . . ." Lord Callanbridge hedged.

"It's better than being stranded in this place," Will argued.

"No, thank you," Lord Callanbridge said. "I'm sure I will get on splendidly here on my own." He looked around at the shabby stalls, filthy yard, and rough characters of the fort. "Splendidly."

"Suit yourself," Will said, doffing his hat. He and James took their leave.

As they were passing through the fort's gates, James remembered that they hadn't found a gift for Sara. He asked Will why he hadn't made an offer on the lord's watch.

"He seemed so forlorn," Will said. "I couldn't take advantage of a man who'd just lost everything he wasn't wearing. It wouldn't have been gentlemanly."

Just then they heard a hallooing coming from behind them. They turned. Lord Callanbridge was running after them.

"Wait!" he called. "Oh, do please wait!"

Will and James looked at each other and smiled. In a minute the lord was standing next to them, panting heavily.

"So, you decided to come on the train with us."

Will clapped the lord on the shoulder. "That fort is no place for a gentleman."

"Quite," Lord Callanbridge said wanly.

And so it was settled. He would join the Stewart train.

SIX

THE CANTER

When James and Will returned to the circle of wagons with their new friend Lord Callanbridge, they had to figure out what to do with him. He had no money, no clothes, and no skills. Who would be willing to take him in?

Then James remembered the widow Loughery.

After her husband had drowned in the South Platte, the widow had struck up a friendship with Pierre Delaroux. The French trapper kept her well supplied with fresh game, so she was never short of food.

But Delaroux was too busy blazing the trail to be of much help otherwise. The Greggs and the Walkers had assisted her at times. She was capable of driving her oxen by herself, and yet she could use a hand.

So Will and James arranged a deal: The widow Loughery would take in Lord Callanbridge. She would cook for him, and she had an extra tent he could sleep in. She had saved her husband's clothing, in hopes of selling it when she got to Oregon City. She agreed to give the lord some of it, so he would have appropriate trail attire.

In exchange, Lord Callanbridge would drive her oxen, and water, feed, and tie them up nights. And he'd do whatever little jobs he was capable of doing.

At first the lord wasn't very proficient at driving the team. But after some coaching by James and Jeremy, he got better at it. The lord was a quick study, and enthusiastic about everything. He was like a man on holiday, eager for new experiences, always carefree and lighthearted. And the widow Loughery was enchanted by his English accent and gracious manners. The arrangement seemed to be satisfactory to everyone.

After crossing the Snake at Fort Boise, the emigrants strayed from the river, following the ruts to the northwest while the river meandered north. After three days they briefly made contact with the river again where it swung to the west.

The place was called Farewell Bend. It was the last the emigrants would see of the Snake, which had been their constant companion for hundreds of miles.

Like the Platte, the Sweetwater, and the Bear before it, the Snake had come to feel like an old friend. Or, James thought, like a schoolteacher. Familiar and comfortable, maybe, but you're never too sorry to say good-bye when the time comes.

James wondered if he'd have to go to school in Oregon. From time to time he'd attended classes in the schoolhouse in Franklin, Pennsylvania, where he'd grown up. But he'd never gone regularly. He was needed on the farm at planting and harvesting times. During the winter there were weeks when the snow was too deep to allow the three-mile walk to town.

Still, James didn't consider his education had suffered. His ma read the Bible aloud almost every night, and he personally had read all of *Robinson Crusoe*, *Gulliver's Travels*, and *Ivanhoe*, which he especially liked. He'd even read some serial excerpts of *Vanity Fair*, a recent best-seller. What more book-learning did a body need?

After all, Cady had gone to school practically every day of her life, and what did she have to show for it? Until James had taught her how, she couldn't ride a horse or fire a gun. She could barely spit straight. *That's where too much schooling will get you*, James thought.

Beyond Farewell Bend lay the Burnt River. Rocky and steep, the trail here was some of the roughest of the whole trip. After two days of following the Burnt, the emigrants were happy to leave it behind too. They struck out between two mountain ridges, toward the Powder River.

To James it seemed as if they were endlessly re-peating themselves—trudging across deserts to reach snow-capped mountains, only to find more desert on the far side. Unloading the wagons and lowering them down steep canyons, then pulling them back up again. Following a river for days on end, leaving it, then following another one. Crossing from one bank to another and then back again. They'd had to ford the Sweetwater River nine times!

Yet there was a feeling of progress. Slowly but surely, they were traversing the continent.

One day, after the train stopped for nooning on the banks of the Powder, James and Cady, along with Bolt, approached Will.

When James had first acquired Bolt, the young horse had been weak and sickly. His owner, Mr. Meacham, was going to put him down. Now Bolt was strong and healthy, and Mr. Meacham had left the train in pursuit of gold in California.

For weeks James had been preparing Bolt for rid-ing. He knew Bolt trusted him, and he wanted to build on that trust. He started by putting a saddle on the horse's back while he watered him.

Then, for several days, he climbed up on a low stool and gently draped his body over Bolt's back. He wanted Bolt to get used to the feeling of a per-son's weight. Bolt snorted nervously at first, but James whispered comforting words to him. The horse calmed down quickly. By the fourth day Bolt

44

allowed James to lift his feet off the stool.

Cady had laughed when she saw James sprawled across his horse's back.

"I thought horses were broken hard, with bucking and kicking," she said. "That's the way the penny papers back in Philadelphia always showed it."

"Some horses do have to be broken that way," James said from atop Bolt's back. "But Bolt trusts me, and I trust him. Why would he want to throw me?"

"That is a better method," Cady admitted. "I'm impressed, James. You're real good with that horse."

James smiled, and went back to murmuring words of assurance to Bolt.

From lying on Bolt's back, James moved to sitting on him. Again Bolt was nervous at first, but soon enough he was walking around and grazing as if he wasn't bothered by the weight at all. After several days of sitting and being taken where Bolt wanted to go, James commenced teaching him commands.

Patiently James taught his horse to respond to words as well as to movements. Bolt was eager to please, and was a fast learner. And James was smart enough not to push him too far. He gave him his way if he seemed intent. James understood that riding was a partnership. A horse that didn't *want* to take commands wasn't a well-trained animal.

After a few weeks, Bolt could walk and trot at three different tempos each, turn to left and right, and even step backward without tripping over his hooves. After each workout, James treated him to a handful of cornmeal or sugar, or some other treat he snuck from the wagon. Pa and Ma didn't relish giving valuable staples to the animals, but they closed their eyes to this small transgression.

All the while James also worked Bolt on the lunge line. At the end of a thirty-foot rope, Bolt walked and trotted in a circle, with James at the center, calling out instructions. Half the time they'd work clockwise, the other half counterclockwise. The lunge line furthered the teachings of the mounted lessons. It also built more trust and understanding between them.

Just the week before, James had introduced the canter—a faster, three-beat pace. He loved watching Bolt's dappled gray shoulders and haunches rocking through the canter, his mane and tail streaming in the air. And he could tell Bolt enjoyed the freedom of movement too—the horse fairly sprang into the air with each stride.

At long last, James felt Bolt was ready to be ridden. Not just walked or trotted slowly in a circle, but really ridden. James had been confident so far that he was training Bolt well. But for the last stage, he wanted a more experienced horseman to assist and advise. And so it was that he, Cady, and Bolt went in search of Will.

They found him lying in the grass, talking to Sara, Jeremy, and Lord Callanbridge. The four had formed a tight friendship.

Sometimes James felt a little left out. After all, he'd been friends with Will first, and it was he who'd spotted the lord at Fort Boise. And of course, his heart still melted at the very sight of Sara. But he had Cady for company, and Bolt and Scraps, so he couldn't complain.

"Howdy, Will, Jeremy. Al." It felt funny calling Lord Callanbridge "Al." James wanted to call him "your highness," or something. He doffed his hat. "How are you, Sara?"

"I'm quite well, thank you."

She was lying on her good hip. James could see the odd angle of her broken leg underneath her blue-checked dress. It choked him up every time he noticed it.

"I was hoping you'd help me with Bolt," James addressed Will. "I aim to ride him before the sun sets. You're welcome too, of course," he added, to Jeremy, Sara, and Lord Callanbridge.

"I'd be happy to help you, Jamie." Will jumped to his feet and slapped the dust off his thighs.

"We were just discussing California," Lord Callanbridge said to James. "They were trying to convince me to travel to San Francisco, of all places. What do you know about this?"

"I know there's a lot of gold talk," James said, "but I've yet to meet anyone who's seen any actual gold." He had a feeling that it was Jeremy and Will, not Sara, who'd been doing most of the talking.

"Dear me," said Lord Callanbridge. "You don't suppose the tales are fraudulent? I've already had more than my share of what you Americans call confidence games—that is the term, is it not?"

"Yeah, that's the term, all right," James said. "You could also call it a swindle."

An awkward silence followed, and James almost regretted trying to shame Will and Jeremy.

"Well now, who wants to see James ride his horse?" Will asked at last.

The friends agreed to come along, and so they all marched to a nearby clearing. In the middle of the grassy open space stood the gigantic stump of a pine tree. James had heard Colonel Stewart explain that in previous years the place had been called Lone Pine Meadow. It had been one of the prettiest spots on the whole Oregon Trail. Then somebody cut the tree down. James would like to have taken a poke at that person.

He mounted Bolt and gently heeled him into a slow trot. By the spring in his horse's step, James could tell that Bolt knew he was being watched. Bolt was a natural performer.

Will had saddled up his own horse, Tempest, and was trotting alongside them. He talked to James, advising him on how best to ease Bolt into the canter. The others shouted encouragement.

Bolt picked up the excitement in their voices. He

was straining at the bit. James held him back, however. He knew Bolt was still a young horse. He didn't want to ask him to do something he couldn't.

Finally James gave a little squeeze with his legs and pushed his hands against Bolt's mane, urging him forward. Bolt broke into an awkward canter, first leading with his left hoof, then with his right. James moved with him, trying to ease him into a steadier gait, talking calmly to him all the while.

After a few minutes Bolt settled into a smooth, rocking pace, not too fast, but enough so that James could feel the wind on his face.

The wind on his face! James had been waiting for this moment for so long—years, it seemed, though really it had been only about four months.

It was a wonderful feeling, riding Bolt across the sagebrush plain, leaving the trail, the wagons, everyone and everything behind. James felt as if he could ride this way forever.

"That's a mighty fine animal, Jamie," Will said. He and Tempest were cantering beside them now.

James wanted to say something, to agree. But all he could do was grin, and laugh, and murmur kind words to Bolt. Bolt picked up the pace, stretching into a fully extended canter. His hooves pounded the packed earth of the plain. His long, graceful strides ate up the land.

"Hey, wait up!" Will urged Tempest into a gallop and was soon riding beside them again. "That's a mighty fine animal," he repeated, "and a mighty *fast* one, too."

The shouts of the others were fading in the distance. Will's big horse had to gallop to keep up with Bolt's canter. The wind whipped at James's face, and the ground raced by in a brown-and-green blur.

James couldn't help himself. Waving his hat in the air, he threw back his head and hollered for wind and speed and freedom. He hollered for the scrawny colt Bolt used to be, and for the powerful horse he'd become.

He hollered for joy.

SEVEN

THE THIRD CONTEST

It was the third week of September. The evenings were cool, and the mornings brought a fine white frost that burned off after an hour. Colonel Stewart had been successful in keeping the emigrants close to schedule. Still, there was no time for resting if they wanted to avoid the early snows of the Cascade Mountains.

The emigrants were still in sagebrush country, as they had been almost since crossing the Missouri border over four months previous.

The familiar plant, its green-gray hue edging into blue, orange, even yellow, had been a valuable source of fuel. James wondered how many months it would take to wash the oily turpentine smell of burning sage out of his hair and clothes.

At the Powder River the sagebrush thinned out, to be replaced by pine forests. The emigrants

51

were entering a new world.

When the train rounded a low mound called Flagstaff Hill, the Blue Mountains came into view for the first time. Colonel Stewart, at the head of the train, called a halt so that every person could take note of the event.

Just as the spring at South Pass had been the first Pacific waters, the Blue Mountains held the first Pacific forests. The emigrants raised a brief cheer, and hastened to move on. The end was so near, now, they didn't want to dally even for a minute.

Soon enough the emigrants forded the Powder River and passed into the valley of the Grande Ronde River. James didn't think he'd ever seen country as beautiful as that of the Grande Ronde, except maybe back home in Pennsylvania.

The streams ran with fat trout of several varieties, as well as salmon so big that James could lift no more than one at a time. Shiny-headed ducks congregated along the banks of ponds, along with geese, beavers, otters, minks, and other animals too numerous to count. James discovered that freshwater clams were tasty steamed or baked, or slurped raw right out of the shell.

Beneath the tall pitch pines and spruce of the forest, wild cherry trees knocked branches with hazelnuts. Fiddlehead ferns with wild strawberries tangled in them blanketed the ground.

The meadows were filled with buttercups and

columbine, primrose and forget-me-nots. Soapberries, huckleberries, and elderberries added their bright fruits to the spattering of color.

James was sure that, given a gun and a fishing pole, he could live forever in the Grande Ronde Valley and never go hungry. And never be anything but happy, either.

"Why don't we stay here?" he asked one day after he and his pa had brought in eight ducks. "We won't ever be short of game, that's for sure."

"It's bountiful country," Pa said. "But we're farmers, not mountain folk. We can live off the land if we have to"—he nodded at the pile of ducks—"but it's not our way. We need society, and society's in Oregon City."

Just then Cady came up to James, holding a big bunch of wildflowers to her nose. "Being a city girl, I need society too. Farm boys like you can get by on the company of cows." She held the flowers out for James to sniff. "But even I have to admit this is awfully nice country."

James inhaled the sweet, spicy odor. "Sometimes cows make for better company than sassy girls."

"That's enough of that, James," his pa said.

"Oh, it's all right, Mr. Gregg." Cady smiled brightly. "I know he doesn't mean it."

I do too mean it, James thought, but he held his tongue.

"When I was picking these flowers," Cady went

on, "I found a raspberry bramble. You want to come see it?"

"I reckon so," James said. He loved raspberries. "You know, sometimes you *are* better company than a cow."

"Why, thank you, James," Cady replied sweetly.

"Don't bump heads with a bear, you two," Pa called after them as they walked away. "They're keen on berry picking this time of year, you know."

"We'll be careful," James assured him.

They fetched baskets from the Greggs' wagon to hold the raspberries. Then Cady led the way, across a broad field of waist-high bluestem grass dotted with wildflowers, to the raspberry patch.

Though raspberries weren't native to the Americas, they were fairly common now along the trail. James commenced digging in with both hands. The bright red fruit was so ripe, all he had to do was shake a stem and the berries would fall into his basket. He lost himself in the rhythm of grasping a branch, stripping it of fruit, and moving on to the next branch. Soon his fingers were stained with sticky red juice.

He couldn't help but stop every few seconds and pop a berry into his mouth. By the red smear around her mouth, he could tell Cady was doing the same.

After an hour of picking in the hot afternoon sun, James was ready to call it quits. His basket was brimful to overflowing, as was his belly. His wrists and forearms bore countless tiny scratches from the sharp thorns of the bushes.

"You about done?" he called over to Cady.

She stepped out from behind a bush, lugging her basket dramatically. "Look at all the berries I got," she said proudly. "I'm probably the best berry picker west of the Rockies." She thrust the basket in front of him.

James lifted his basket to compare. Hers was about three quarters full. His could hardly hold another berry. He snickered lowly.

"Let me see!" she snapped. A scowl crossed her face as she examined the baskets. "It's obvious my basket is bigger than yours. That's why yours looks fuller."

"You won't stop, will you?" He shook his head and sighed. "The baskets are alike and you know it. I just picked more berries than you did; it's as simple as that. I can swim better, shoot straighter, and run faster than you can. Now I can pick berries quicker too. Face it. You're never going to beat me in anything."

Cady's eyes fairly popped out of her head. "Why, you're nothing but a . . . a . . ." She couldn't even come up with the words, she was so sore. "I was eating them as I went along!" she screeched. "That's why you have more in your basket!"

"Oh, law!" James was really enjoying himself now. "As if I wasn't. I probably had twice as many as you did. On top of everything else, I'm better at *eating* berries than you are."

"You think so?"

James nodded, smirking.

"You think so?" Cady repeated. "We'll just see about that. I'll match you berry for berry." She dumped her basket at his feet. "Start eating," she commanded.

James sat cross-legged in the grass. What had been a heaping mound of raspberries was reduced now to a mere two dozen stray berries.

From the start, he'd chosen smaller ones. Unfortunately, Cady had caught on to the scheme and had chosen smaller ones too. Now, when both of them needed mercy, only the biggest ones remained.

Grimly he reached for a berry and shoved it between his teeth. He mashed it with his tongue and, fighting back an urge to gag, forced himself to swallow. He felt ill—bloated, woozy, and queasy. If he never tasted raspberries again for as long as he lived, it would be too soon.

Cady sat opposite him, a blank look on her face. She picked up a berry and placed it on her bright red tongue. She closed her eyes and worked her jaws. Her upper lip twitched as she gulped the berry down.

James didn't know if he could stomach another. Luckily, it was getting late in the day. The air was

56

cooler now, and the sun was approaching the horizon fast. They should be heading back to camp soon. Probably Cady would agree to a truce.

"Maybe we should call it a tie," James offered. It was the first time either of them had spoken since the contest began an hour ago. "Our folks'll be expecting us."

"You're giving up?" Cady sneered. "Ready to admit I'm a better berry eater?"

"I'm not giving up," James said. Coldly he searched the pile. There had to be a small one left. But no. Only great big fat ripe ones awaited him. He imagined the juice bursting into his mouth, running all over his teeth and tongue, dripping down his throat.

His stomach lurched, and he turned away. He couldn't bear to look at another berry.

"Ha!" Cady shouted triumphantly. "Can't take it, can you, James? Watch this!"

Out of the corner of his eye, he saw her scoop up a handful of berries and stuff them in her mouth.

"De-rishush," she declared through the half-chewed mush.

"Uhhh . . ." James groaned. If he didn't start walking soon, he was going to lose what he'd eaten. He stood up, extending his hand to her. "You win."

She took his hand, and he pulled her to her feet. "I just wanted to hear you say it," she said.

James looked distastefully at the bright red

berries remaining in his basket. "You reckon we ought to take these back to camp?" he asked.

Cady blanched. "I suppose so."

Carrying the basket, but trying hard not to look at its contents, James headed for the field of wildflowers. Cady was right behind. Halfway across the grassy field, he realized she was no longer following him.

He turned. She was nowhere in sight. "Cady?" he called.

No answer.

"Cady!" He dropped his basket and started back toward the raspberry bramble.

Trotting through the waist-high grass, he called out for her again. Still no answer. What had become of her? Maybe a bear had come along, as his pa had warned. Or some other wild animal. There was no telling what sort of danger she could be in.

James stopped short at the sight of Cady's checkered blue dress in the middle of the footpath, twenty feet away. She was on her hands and knees. Had she been bitten by a snake? Why hadn't she cried out?

"Cady?" James said, approaching cautiously. Then he burst into gales of laughter. "Oh ho, look who it is! The champion berry eater brought low!" He slapped his hat on his knee and laughed some more.

Cady was doubled over, clutching her gut and coughing. In front of her was a wide, shockingly red pool—the former contents of her stomach. She hacked and gagged as the last few drops dribbled out of her mouth.

"Hey, are you all right?" James asked, serious now. She might really be sick.

"I'm fine," she muttered. "Right as rain."

She coughed several more times, then wiped her mouth on the hem of her dress. "You're not to tell a soul about this, James Gregg."

"And if I do?" James snickered. "If I tell everyone in the train—what are you going to do about it?"

She rose unsteadily to her feet, brushed down her dress, and drew herself erect. "A gentleman doesn't purposely strive to humiliate a lady, James Gregg," she said with great dignity.

Her words stung him. Though he'd had no trouble watching her retch, he couldn't look at her now.

"If you utter a word of this to anyone," she said, "I will never speak to you ever again for as long as I live. And you know I mean it, James Gregg."

Indeed, he knew she did. His teasing had gone far enough for one day. So without another word, he offered his hand, and she took it. In this manner they made their way back to camp.

And though he made her carry his basket of berries, he told the others that it was she who had picked them.

EIGHT

THE FREEMAN

James regretted leaving the valley of the Grande Ronde, especially since the Blue Mountains loomed ahead. The climb to the main pass was neither steep nor particularly dangerous—at least compared to other parts of the trail. But while the climb wasn't steep, it was long. The main divide was several thousand feet up.

Frost formed on the ground every morning now, and even at midday the air had a bite to it. James knew it was partly because they were so high up in the mountains. But it was also due to the time of year—autumn was fast approaching.

The westernmost saddle of the Blue Mountains was called Deadman Pass. No one, not even Colonel Stewart or Pierre Delaroux, knew why. James had some ideas, all of them lurid, so he kept them to himself.

From the summit of Deadman Pass, the emigrants could see the Umatilla River valley stretched out some five miles below them. After a rapid descent out of the Blue Mountains, they camped by the banks of the Umatilla, thankful for the low elevation and another obstacle overcome.

Ma fried a mess of corn cakes, and the Greggs and Walkers shared stewed rabbit with dumplings.

Will and Sara joined them for dinner, as did the widow Loughery, Pierre Delaroux, and Lord Callanbridge. James was thankful he was no longer expected to wash everyone's plates. While he never teased Cady about the raspberry incident, he took every chance to remind her whose fault it was that they'd lost the contest with his pa and brother.

The food was warm and savory, and everyone ate his or her fill. Dessert was raspberry pie, made from a basketful that Ma and Elizabeth had picked while coming down out of the mountain. James and Cady politely declined.

Pa broke out his fiddle and played a little tune, and the group sang sad songs of days gone by and cheerful ones of times to come.

Near the edge of the light from the fire, James lay snug under his buffalo-skin blanket. He looked up at the stars twinkling in the black, black sky and let his mind wander while his stomach did its work. He thought of Scott and wondered where his friend might be. Waiting at St. Peter's gate for the word to come on in, or already in heaven, sitting by the right hand of God? He thought of riding Bolt, what he'd teach him next. He thought of Sara, resting now in Will's arms on the other side of the fire. Of his sister Elizabeth, who like a bean sprout seemed to grow taller every day—

Suddenly he was aware of a rustling in the darkness beyond the fire. A cold feeling of fear came over him.

Scraps began barking loudly, and James's pa dropped the fiddle. He leveled a rifle in the direction of the noise. James was astonished—he hadn't even realized Pa had the gun handy.

Everyone around the campfire hushed. The only sounds were the crackling of the fire, Scraps growling lowly, and the crickets trilling in the distance.

Then a small cough came out of the darkness.

"Who's there?" Pa said calmly but forcefully. "Show yourself."

James's heart was in his throat. Was it Indians? So far the train had had no trouble with them, but James had heard the rumors—midnight rampages, scalpings. The women kidnapped and kept as slaves, the children held prisoner until they forgot they weren't Indians themselves.

Last year, not five miles north of where they were camped, the Whitman Mission had been wiped out by marauding Indians. Or so folks claimed.

"Show yourself or I fire!" Pa said.

The figure of a man, his hands raised in a gesture of peace, stepped out of the darkness and into the edge of the dancing firelight. He was a tall man in a broad-brimmed hat and a long duster. Not an Indian.

James relaxed a little. Still, there was no telling what kind of mischief a man wandering the wilderness alone might be up to.

The man took another step, into brighter light. James squinted to make out his features.

"I'd be much obliged," the man said slowly, stepping forward, "if you'd be so kind as to allow me and my wife to share your fire."

James realized with a start that the fellow was black. The last black men James had seen were slaves working the docks in Independence, Missouri.

"My name's Samuel Gregg." Pa put his gun on the ground, and the other man lowered his hands. "Set yourself down."

A woman stepped out of the darkness. She took the stranger's hand.

James couldn't believe his eyes.

The woman was white.

James could tell by the expression on his pa's face that he was as surprised as anyone.

"Name's Jonas Prudhomme." The man extended his hand, and Pa grasped it. "This is my wife, Aurora Prudhomme."

"Pleased to make your acquaintance," Mrs. Prudhomme said, curtsying slightly.

No one said anything for a moment.

"Well, Mr. Prudhomme," Ma said, "you must be

famished, out on a night like this. Why don't you and the missus make yourselves comfortable by the fire. We have rabbit stew, still warm." She smiled. "I'll make sure you each get a nice fat dumpling."

While further introductions were made, and Mr. and Mrs. Prudhomme settled near the fire, James looked at the familiar faces around it.

Elizabeth was playing with Scraps, her loud giggling broken only by even louder yawns. A little sleepy, perhaps, but seemingly unaware of anything unusual.

The others—Delaroux and the widow, the Walkers, the lord—were subdued. James guessed that, like himself, they were curious, perhaps a bit perplexed.

James met Jeremy's eye. What were they to make of this pair? James had never met a couple like them—a white woman and a man of color, *married*. To *each other*.

Sara was chatting with Mrs. Prudhomme now. They seemed completely at ease. Sara, James thought, had a way with people.

Only Will looked upset. A frown creased his face, and his dark eyes burned with agitation. He was staring at Mr. Prudhomme as if the man were a ghost.

"Tell us, Mr. Prudhomme," Pa said.

"Call me Jonas, please," the man broke in. "Mrs. Gregg, this is mighty tasty stew. Downright heavenly."

"Why, thank you, Jonas. And do call us Sam and Amelia."

Mr. Prudhomme nodded, smiling.

"Jonas, what brings you to this godforsaken place at such an hour?" Pa glanced at Mrs. Walker. "Pardon my French." Then he glanced at Delaroux. "Er, language."

"We've been traveling for months now, living off the land," Mr. Prudhomme said. "Two weeks ago we were camped at Malheur Lake. By next week I expect we'll have reached the mouth of the Snake. That's if the Nez Perce and Walla-Wallapoos give us no trouble."

James recognized the names as Indian tribes.

"You'll be passing near the site of the Whitman Massacre," Pa observed. "Are you sure that's wise?"

"Wise? Maybe not." Mr. Prudhomme shrugged. "But I don't put much stock in tales about Indians. I've met plenty of them and haven't been massacred yet. Besides, I hear tell there wasn't any massacre—more of a battle. And it wasn't the Indians who started it, either."

"Well, that wouldn't surprise me," Pa admitted. "Still, you're mighty daring to travel alone, with no animals—"

"Oh, we have a mule," said Mrs. Prudhomme. "He's yonder by your wagon."

"Why didn't you say so?" said Pa. "Tie him up with our oxen, so he doesn't wander off."

"No need for that. Old Tim's not going anywhere." Mr. Prudhomme gave a deep, rolling laugh. "No, he doesn't go anywhere I don't make him."

Pa and the others laughed along with him.

"And where are you fixing on making him go?" Pa asked. "The mouth of the Snake is no proper destination, if you don't mind my saying so."

"We'll be putting the Snake behind us soon enough," said Mrs. Prudhomme. "Along with the rest of the Oregon Territory. This country's no good for us any longer."

James didn't understand. Why would anyone choose to leave the United States and its territories?

"You see, I was born in New Orleans," Mr. Prudhomme said, "and was apprenticed as a tanner. I've been a free man my whole life. Never called another man master. And never owned a man either, though I had the means. I ran my own shop, and my saddles were known all up the river as the finest in Louisiana.

"But when Aurora and I met, and fell in love . . ." A dark look passed over Mr. Prudhomme's face that spoke of many troubles.

"Well, it was time to move on," Mrs. Prudhomme finished for him.

"Why don't you stay in the Oregon Territory, Mr. Prudhomme?" James asked. He knew the South had slaves, and he could imagine how difficult life there would be for a free man of color. But the Oregon Territory didn't allow slavery. Everyone in Oregon was free.

Mr. Prudhomme shook his head slowly. "I don't see as I have much choice, son. There are no slaves in Oregon, it's true. But some years ago the Oregon legislature banned Negroes from settling in the territory."

James was flabbergasted. He'd never heard of that law before. It didn't seem fair.

"We aim to settle in Canada." Mrs. Prudhomme sighed. "And I'm sorry it has to be so."

"I love my country as much as any man," her husband added. "And I'd gladly die defending the Union. But there's no place in the South for Aurora and me, and the North isn't much different. Now the frontier is closed to us too."

The little group around the fire was silent while Mr. Prudhomme's words sank in. James was troubled by the injustice of it all. No one, not even a territorial legislator, had the right to tell a man where he could or couldn't live.

The West was supposed to be open to all comers, James thought. Every man was free to chart his own destiny. At least that's what he'd always been told. He was now beginning to realize that it wasn't always true.

James's ma commenced stowing away the tin plates, and the others headed back to their wagons. Pa insisted that the Prudhommes sleep that night by the Greggs' fire before they set out early the next morning.

When James awoke the next morning, the Prudhommes had already gone. He wanted to talk to someone about the unusual visitors of the night before.

James found Will harnessing the Teagues' oxen. As James chattered excitedly about the Prudhommes, Will loaded the yoke on the animals' backs. James noticed his friend seemed quiet, even testy, this morning.

"What's troubling you, Will?" he asked.

"It's the Prudhommes," Will said.

"Oh, I know. It's a shame, them leaving the country, and he loving it so much and all." James spat on the ground. "Who gave those legislator fellows the right to say who can move to Oregon and who can't?"

"It's a shame, I agree," Will said. "But that's not what's bothering me."

James raised his eyebrows.

"You know I left Virginia because I couldn't stand the sight of a man in chains," Will said.

James nodded.

"When I was little," Will continued, "my daddy taught me to judge folks according to their character, not by their clothes or houses or clubs. 'You know a gentleman,' he said, 'not by the shine on his shoes, but by the shine on his deeds.' When I had grown up some, I decided my daddy was an old jackass—teaching me not to judge others by their looks, and then enslaving them on the basis of the color of their skin! And I didn't mind telling my daddy what I thought of him and his homilies, too."

Will ran his hand through his dark hair. "Now, I'm not sure, but I've been the jackass all along. When Mr. Prudhomme introduced his wife . . . why, Jamie, I'm too ashamed to admit what was going through my head."

James didn't want Will to think he was the only one who'd had such thoughts. "I'll admit I was surprised to see . . ." James didn't know how to put it politely. "A mixed marriage, I gather it's called."

"Surprised?" Will gave a short laugh. "Jamie, where I come from, that kind of surprise'll have you hanging from the nearest tree limb right quick."

"It's not real common where I come from either," James said. "I reckon that's why they're going to Canada."

Will looked thoughtfully at James. "I reckon so."

"You're being too hard on yourself, Will," James said seriously. "You were brought up a certain way, and you can't snap your fingers and hope to change. Sometimes a body just needs time to adjust. The important thing is that you're trying. You can't expect to live up to your own highest standards every moment of the day."

"I *can* expect it," Will replied.

"Then you're going to keep disappointing yourself," James said quietly. "And those you love."

NINE

CAMAS AND KISSES

For three days in a row, it rained from sunup to sundown and didn't let up nights, either. The trail twice crossed the Umatilla—once to the north side, and then back over to the south. What was normally an easy fording was made difficult by the river swollen with rain.

In those few minutes when the clouds lifted, the emigrants could see the Blue Mountains, now capped with white. They'd been fortunate to get through before the snows came. James hoped they'd be as lucky in the Cascades.

Walking through the rain was a misery, but at least the misery was shared. No one enjoyed it. The people were muddy and cold, not to mention soaked to the bone. The animals had to struggle for footing on the slick trail. Wagons bogged down in the mud.

At night James's pa managed to build a smoky fire out of wet timber, and everyone, human and animal, huddled around it and soaked up the soothing warmth.

At the start of the journey, the emigrants had had to take great care in tying up the work animals at night. But after almost five months of pulling and plodding, they were completely broken in spirit. The oxen were about as likely to run off as to fly away. And most of the horses were the same. All they desired was rest.

Under James's special care and treatment, though, Bolt had thrived. Not that he wanted to run off. But the fifteen miles of walking every day had served to build up his stamina. The extra treats—handfuls of sugar, corn mash, dried apples—kept his coat glossy and his eyes bright. There was no better-looking horse on the train.

By the time the rain let up, the emigrants had left the Umatilla River behind them. They were rolling due west across sandy—now muddy—flats. Colonel Stewart explained that the Columbia River was but ten miles to the north.

"Why don't we just head on up and meet it," James asked, "and float the rest of the way?"

"If you saw the Columbia River gorge," Colonel Stewart answered, laughing, "you'd know the reason. That river isn't navigable by anything but salmon for another eighty miles."

It was nooning, and all up and down the train folks were airing out their wet clothes and belongings in the suddenly dry air. James helped his ma and Elizabeth string a line between their wagon and the Walkers', to hang laundry on. They didn't have much clothing—James had two pairs of overalls and three shirts. But every inch of what they had was soaked.

James was watching Elizabeth pin up one of Jeremy's handkerchiefs when he noticed some Indians coming toward the train. His heart started pounding hard, and he ordered Elizabeth inside the wagon. Even after having met so many friendly Indians, the sight of them still made James edgy.

They were a motley group of about twenty individuals, mostly men, though a few were women or children. Several of the men rode horses. But the thing that struck James was that a number of the older men had foreheads that were smooth and very flat, and oddly elongated. They looked as if their heads had been put in vises and mashed.

Though the Indians appeared to be unarmed, James went to alert his pa.

Pa had seen them coming, though, and was already on his way, along with Colonel Stewart, Pierre Delaroux, and several other men.

James ran after them. "May I meet with the Indians too, Pa?"

Pa shot a look at Delaroux, and the big trapper nodded his assent.

"Most of these folks are Cayuse," Pa explained. "They live in the Blue Mountains, and all over these parts. Colonel Stewart told me there's a village not far from the trail—fenced-in fields where they grow corn, potatoes, pumpkins. They have right sturdy longhouses fit for the best society."

"What about the ones with the flat foreheads?" James whispered. "What's wrong with them?" He knew they couldn't understand English. But still, it wasn't polite to ask questions about people's appearance in their presence.

"Those fellows aren't Cayuses," Pa said. "They're what you call Flathead Indians, from the west. The colonel said we'll see more of them around Fort Vancouver, and in Oregon City. They look that way because their tribe used to bind boards to their babies' heads. They thought it made 'em look more impressive."

James had to admit these older men were impressive. "Didn't it hurt?"

"Aw, no," Pa said. "The babies just grew into it. But you don't see many young folks with the flattened heads anymore, at least not according to Mr. Delaroux. The old ways are dying out. Some of these Indians are even taking to white folks' dress."

James had noticed that a number of Cayuses in the group had on breeches, and one Flathead wore a top hat. With the tall hat perched on his long head, he was almost comical, James thought—but no more so than the white trappers who wore feathers in their hair back at Fort Boise.

Introductions were made mainly with hand gestures and smiles. Then the trading began in earnest. James could never get over how, despite all he'd read back east about wild Indian attacks, the Indians he'd met were always peaceful. All they wanted to do was trade, then escort the train off their lands. About the most aggressive thing he'd ever seen an Indian do was try to insist on a bad deal—and that was nothing compared to the way some white traders dealt with each other.

Pa counted out twenty fishhooks, placing them in the palm of one of the Cayuses. The man offered a stack of what looked like fallen brown cakes. Each of the half-dozen cakes was about eight inches across and a little over an inch thick.

"What're those?" James asked.

"These are called camas cakes," Pa said. "They're made out of a root vegetable that's something like an onion, only sweeter. I hear tell the Cayuses fairly live on them in the winter."

James examined the cakes. They smelled delicious—a little like toasted figs.

"This here fellow," Pa began, nodding at another Cayuse he was trading with, "has fresh camas. Mr. Delaroux told me the Cayuses dig a hole, put a hot stone in the bottom, throw some camas in, then cover it all with dirt and green grass. After a couple of hours, they dig the camas up and have a feast." He eyed his son. "Would you like to try cooking camas in the ground? For ten more fishhooks, we could get a basketful. Or we could get plain potatoes."

James considered. He remembered how good the salmon poached in the hot spring had been. Why not camas roasted in a hole in the ground? "Let's take the camas," he said.

Pa smiled. "Let's."

That afternoon James prepared dinner. As his pa instructed, he built a fire and heated up a large stone. Then he dug a hole, rolled the stone into it, tossed in the camas and some earth, and covered it all with fresh grass.

"I never thought I'd see the day when my son Jamie wanted to take over the cooking," Ma declared. "It surely is true that the West works wonders on a boy."

James grinned. He only hoped the result would be edible. If not, he always had the camas cakes to fall back on.

After two hours, he dug the camas out. They were black on the outside from the roasting. Hoping they weren't black all the way through, James peeled one with his knife. Cream colored and sweet smelling, the camas was still warm on the inside. It was perfect.

"You're a good cook, James," Cady said that night. "I never would have guessed it." She took another bite of camas and gave him an admiring smile. "Tasty."

"Thanks." James blushed fiercely. He wasn't used to accepting compliments, especially from girls. "It was the Indians' idea," he said modestly.

For the next several days, the train made slow progress. No longer having to slog through rain, the emigrants were now faced with yet another sandy desert. The country here was all shifting sand dunes, like pictures James had seen of Arabia. He wondered if camels would have been more able to walk this part of the trail. The oxen sure were having a hard time of it.

Between stretches of sandy flats were rocky canyons and buttes. It seemed to James that if it wasn't mud flats, it was sand flats. If it wasn't sand flats, it was rocky ascents. And the only thing worse than a rocky ascent was a rocky descent.

At the high places, the emigrants could make out in the far-off distance the Cascade Range. Like huge twins, the white conical domes of Mount Hood and Mount Adams flashed on the horizon. The Columbia River split the Cascade Range, running between the two giant peaks.

The Columbia was the last great river before Oregon City. Reaching it marked the last phase of the journey. In the last phase, the train would split up. While the men took the animals overland south around Mount Hood, the women would raft with the wagons down the river.

One day Colonel Stewart halted the train at the crest of a hill. He bade the emigrants come forward.

What could it be? James wondered, running to the front. Surely it was some kind of trouble. . . .

The colonel waited till all the members of the train were gathered around him. Then he pointed west, and made a simple announcement: "My friends, the Columbia River!"

Everyone looked to where he was pointing. Below, some three miles off, was the silvery thread of a river. The Columbia, Gateway to the Pacific, lay before them like a promised gift at last delivered.

They whooped and hollered and tossed their hats in the air, grabbed one another and kissed and cried, so happy were they to have gained the First View.

James found himself hugging his ma, swinging little Elizabeth around him, pounding Jeremy on the back. The widow Loughery placed a big wet slobbery kiss on his cheek. Pierre Delaroux slapped him on the shoulder in celebration. James hugged everyone he could lay his hands on—Will, Mr. Jennington, Sara, even Lord Callanbridge.

Laughing, James spun around, and who was in

his arms but Cady. She grappled him around the chest and pressed her head to his shoulder. She was gripping him so tight, he could barely breathe. He had no choice but to hug her back.

Then, lifting her face, she planted her lips on his.

James was so astonished, he didn't know what to do. So he closed his eyes and puckered. After a moment, Cady pulled her lips away. James opened his eyes. She grinned broadly at him, then turned and disappeared into the crowd.

She'd kissed him.

On the lips!

It was only for a few seconds, but it was still a kiss.

He hadn't kissed her back.

Much.

All right, so he'd puckered a little. Did that count as kissing back? James wasn't sure. Probably Cady would think it did. She would probably blame him for the whole thing. And he hadn't even enjoyed it.

Had he?

He wasn't sure.

He wasn't sure of much of anything. Was he angry? He tried to be, but had to admit he wasn't. Mostly he was stunned.

He hoped no one had seen it happen, especially not Jeremy. His brother would never let him hear the end of it.

Not that it was shameful or anything. Cady was a

sight prettier than old Missy had ever been, anyway.

James wiped his mouth on his sleeve and went back to hollering about the Columbia. But his heart was no longer in the celebration.

He couldn't stop thinking about the kiss—and Cady.

TEN

THE BRIDGE TO HEAVEN

The next day the Stewart train came to The Dalles of the Columbia. The Dalles was a series of rock falls that lay across the river. Between two huge rocks the water came shooting out, spraying white foam into a black pool. Even Devil's Gate of the Sweetwater didn't thunder so, James thought.

Below The Dalles, ferry services rafted some emigrants the rest of the way to Oregon City. Three families—the Batkins, the Skoneckis, and the McElroys—had left the train a month ago to follow the California Trail. Eli Meacham and his wife had gone before them. Here, at The Dalles, the train split up for good.

Women, children, and wagons would be loaded onto rafts and floated down the Columbia to Fort Vancouver. A few miles past Fort Vancouver, the

Willamette River flowed into the Columbia from the south. There the rafts would turn up the Willamette, journeying about twenty-five miles to Oregon City.

James understood that it wasn't an easy trip. Part of the Columbia—a stretch of falls called the Cascades—wasn't navigable, so the women would have to make a portage of about a mile. That meant they would have to get off the rafts and carry their possessions.

But all in all, the river route from The Dalles to Oregon City was easier than the overland route.

Horses, let alone oxen, sheep, and the other animals in the train, could not be rafted down a rough river. Their nerves couldn't take it. So the men had to take them to Oregon City by land.

In the earliest days of the Oregon Trail, the land route from The Dalles had clung to the Columbia River, skirting north of Mount Hood. But two years ago, in 1846, a new way, the Barlow Road, had been discovered. It swung around south of Mount Hood. The distance to Oregon City was about the same, and the trail was slightly less treacherous. Still, it did cut awfully close to Mount Hood—the main pass was nearly as high as the South Pass of the Rockies.

After splitting up, the men and women of the Stewart train would come together again in Oregon City. There they would begin their new lives.

The Stewart train had been fortunate so far. Thanks to wise leadership from the colonel and Pierre Delaroux, only five of the original fifty-eight members of the train had perished. Many trains lost one third, or even half, their members.

James dearly wished for no more deaths, now they were all so close.

The emigrants were camped near The Dalles this last night, within earshot of the falls. In the morning James and the other men would escort the women and wagons to a place called Chenowith Creek, and there bid them farewell. Then the men would backtrack four miles to the Barlow Road and start walking south.

It was a peaceful night. The thundering of the falls in the distance was like a lulling whisper. Little did the emigrants relish the morrow's separation, and their spirits were low.

On this last night they were gathered around a single large bonfire. Some were singing softly, and others were discussing days on the trail gone by. Mostly there was silence, however, and a growing sadness.

James sat with his family and the Walkers. He took care to keep Jeremy and Elizabeth between himself and Cady. He wanted plenty of space between them, in case she was in the kissing mood again.

Pa and Ma, along with the widow Loughery, were discussing the Prudhommes.

"It's a crying shame," Ma said. "Fine people like them, having to flee their own country because of others' ignorance."

"A body has to face the consequences of his actions," Pa said evenly. "Rightly or not, most folks don't approve of a marriage like the Prudhommes'."

"I think it's romantic," the widow Loughery declared. "A man and a woman in love, insisting on being together despite all the forces conspiring to keep them apart."

The widow shot a kindly look at Pierre Delaroux. James would almost have sworn that the burly trapper blushed in response.

"I agree with you," Cady said to the widow. "Take two people who are very different. Say one's from the city, and the other's from the country. When those two get together, there's nothing more romantic in the whole world."

Now it was James's turn to blush. He was glad more than ever that Jeremy and Elizabeth separated himself from Cady.

Then Ma and Pa, along with the widow Loughery and Mrs. Walker, commenced singing hymns—"How Firm a Foundation, Ye Saints of the Lord" and "We Gather Together to Ask the Lord's Blessing." When their voices died, the mournful silence came back again.

The lonesomeness in the air was so sharp, James felt he was going to bust out in tears if someone didn't do something quick.

Thankfully, Will decided to speak up. "Back home in Virginia," he said loudly, "the land is thick with wags. And I've listened to my share of them. But for my money, there's none quicker with a quip or taller with a tale than one of our very own." He turned to the colonel, who was sitting nearby. "I've tried to best you in witcracks and whoppers, sir. I'm man enough to concede that you're the best story-teller in this train." Will tipped his hat gracefully. "Do honor us with another tale, this last night we're all together."

The colonel gave a little smile and knocked the ashes out of his pipe, sending them sparking into the air. Then he gazed into the campfire for a very long stretch.

"You know, I've spent some time in this territory, traded up Fort Vancouver way," he began. "The trappers in these parts live cheek-by-jowl with Indians. Stories get swapped right along with pelts and tobacco."

The colonel looked out beyond the fire, toward the low murmuring of the falls. "You hear that sound?" he asked. "The roaring of The Dalles?"

James, along with the others around the fire, nodded.

"The Indians tell a story about The Dalles. They say heaven and earth came together here once long ago."

The colonel paused for a moment. The sound of water rushing through The Dalles filled up the quiet.

"Long ago," the colonel said, "a great bridge spanned heaven and earth. The People of the Sky used it to come down and visit the People of the Earth. The Sky People brought gifts. They taught the Earth People many good things to know—how to grow pumpkins and corn, how to catch salmon, how to cook camas in the ground."

James smiled. How to cook camas in the ground was a good thing to know.

"The Sky People lived in peace and harmony with the Earth People," the colonel went on, "crossing the bridge to heaven as they pleased. But the Sky People did not allow the Earth People to use the bridge. And so there were those among the People of the Earth who were unhappy."

" 'Why should we not visit heaven?' they asked one another. 'Why do the Sky People come and go as free as birds, while we are stuck down here like tortoises?' "

Colonel Stewart paused again, and again the moment was filled by the sound of distant water shooting through The Dalles.

"So the Earth People assembled a mighty war party," he said. "Ten thousand braves, each with a hundred arrows, every arrow tipped with a deadly point. The braves would take the bridge to heaven by force, and show the Sky People that they were not to be trifled with.

"Up in heaven, the Sky People merely shook their heads in sorrow at the folly of those below. They warned the Earth People, 'Do not attempt such foolishness. You are made for the earth, not the sky.'

"But the warriors down below wouldn't listen. They took their shiny arrows and attacked the bridge. Howling and yelling and whooping and crying, they raced onto the bridge, all ten thousand of them."

The colonel raised his hands up like a preacher, and shook his fists at the sky. "And then came a terrible splitting cracking rolling thunder," he said, his own voice rising. "No sound more terrible had ever been heard before on earth. The bridge to heaven gave way, collapsing beneath the anger and spite and foolishness of the ten thousand braves, taking the warriors with it to their doom."

The colonel had been fairly shouting while he described the fall of the bridge to heaven. Now he whispered, "And since that day, the Sky People no longer walk among the folks down here on earth. They no longer bring gifts, or teach us new things, or mingle in our affairs. The fallen bridge to heaven you can still see in the rocks of The Dalles now strewn across the Columbia. You can still hear the echo of the great thundering collapse in the roar of the water. And if you listen closely, beneath the sound of the thundering you can hear the faint cries of the dead warriors who dared attack heaven."

The colonel was finished, his story over. In the quiet that followed, James heard the roaring of The Dalles now louder than ever.

Suddenly Colonel Stewart clapped his hands, breaking the spell. "Well, I best turn in." He rose abruptly. "We have a big day tomorrow, packing up the wagons and seeing the women off. I'll bid you good night, gentlemen." He tipped his hat with the big white feather and smiled. "Ladies."

Then he disappeared into the darkness.

"That Colonel Stewart sure knows how to spin a yarn," Will said.

"'Deed he does," Pa agreed. "And he chooses his stories well. Tonight he told one about a terrible separation." Pa took Ma's hand. "On the morrow we face our own separation."

James had noticed the same thing. He wondered how much of Colonel Stewart's tale had been Indian legend, and how much was made up to fit the colonel's devices.

The little party around the fire began breaking up, families straying off for one last night together.

As James lay beneath his heavy buffalo blanket, he listened to the far-off rushing of The Dalles. Its pulsing and pounding filled the space around him. And beneath it, James thought he could make out the stifled cries of ten thousand braves falling to their deaths.

ELEVEN

A RUSTLE IN THE LEAVES

Dawn came cold and frosty as the emigrants gathered at Chenowith Creek. Their breath rose out of their mouths and noses in long white streams. The rising sun glinted off the blue Columbia. Working to load the wagons onto rafts, the emigrants soon forgot about the cold.

James was glad for the activity. He ran from wagon to wagon, unharnessing oxen, hauling yokes, shouldering wheels. He kept himself busy, for the busier he was, the less he thought about saying farewell to his ma and sister. And Sara. And Cady, of course.

"You don't have to make such a big show of being in a hurry," Cady said, approaching him. A wicked scowl bunched her eyebrows together. "I can tell you can't wait to be clear of the womenfolk."

"What are you going on about now?" James asked.

"You get to cross a mountain and have more adventures, while I'm stuck with the *ladies* on the raft."

"After all our walking, a raft ride sounds tempting," James said. "If I had my druthers—"

"You'd have all the adventures," Cady interrupted him. "I can climb any mountain you can, James Gregg. And I don't need any raft to take me to Oregon City." She spun on her heels and stomped off.

James crossed his eyes at her back. What a sorehead she was sometimes. The only reason she wanted to climb the Cascades was that that's what he was doing. If he were going by raft, she'd want to go that way.

Putting Cady out of mind, James went back to work. He leaped among the rafts, grabbing ropes and strapping down wagons.

"Hold on, son," his pa said at last. He patted the patch of bank where he was resting, and James sat down next to him. "You know, you can always tell a man who's not used to hard labor. He's the one who's in a rush. A good worker knows to pace himself."

James had watched his pa working the fields back in Pennsylvania. Pa always moved at a deliberate, steady pace—no unnecessary motions, no wasted energy. He seemed to go slowly, and yet he always finished a task quicker than James ever could.

"I reckon I'm too excited to slow down," James said.

"Well, now, that's understandable." Pa laid his

hand on James's shoulder. "I'd do the same, except old fellows like myself have to partake of our exertions in small helpings. You go knock yourself out if you need to."

"Thanks." James grinned. "And you're not that old."

He went back to rushing around. As fewer and fewer tasks remained, his panicky feeling grew and grew. He truly dreaded saying farewell.

Finally the moment came. The oxen, free of their heavy yokes, stood tethered on the bank, along with the horses and other animals. The wagons were loaded on the rafts.

Strapped together at the landing, the rafts were a maze of confusion. In addition to the piles of possessions, trunks, wagons, women, and children from the Stewart train, a number of trappers and traders, down from the Cascades for the winter, added to the bustle.

There were many tearful good-byes. James hopped from raft to raft, seeking out Ma and Elizabeth.

"James, over here!" his sister called. Ma was next to her.

He ran to them, and was smothered in a big sloppy hug from the both of them.

"You be a good boy," Ma told him. "Don't give your father any trouble."

"You know I won't," James said.

Ma smiled. "I know."

James went in search of others to say good-bye to.

Mrs. Jennington and Mrs. Teague were weeping together over their husbands. Little Prudence Sundstrom was bawling loudly at being separated from her papa and his loyal oxen. The widow Loughery was blowing her nose over Lord Callanbridge and Pierre Delaroux.

As part of his arrangement with the widow, Lord Callanbridge was driving her oxen to Oregon City, rather than taking the easier river route.

"I thank you for your confidence in my abilities as a teamster," Lord Callanbridge said to the widow. "I shall not fail you."

Mr. Delaroux's contract with the train required only that he guide the emigrants to The Dalles. From here, Colonel Stewart alone could find the way. But Mr. Delaroux had volunteered to continue on with the men to Oregon City.

"I have become quite fond of all my friends," he said, grinning sheepishly. "I am hesitant to part from them."

James wondered if it wasn't in fact a certain widow he'd grown fond of, and was reluctant to leave.

Among all the folks hugging and weeping and saying good-bye, James found Will and Sara standing on one of the rafts. They were holding hands, looking miserable.

When Will noticed James approaching, he quickly kissed Sara on the cheek and tipped his hat. "It's only a week before I'll see you again, so I'll not say good-bye." He kissed her one more time, turned on his heel, and left.

Sara turned to James. "I'll be seeing you in a week too." She forced a smile.

James looked in her big dark eyes, now all trembly with tears. "What's troubling you, Miss Sara?" he asked.

"Oh, Jamie," she said. "I know you don't believe me, but it's in every word he says—'only a week' before we're together again. I know he wishes it was more."

James sighed. Maybe Sara was right. Maybe Will didn't love her anymore. After all, Will was convinced that she didn't love him. He'd said so himself. How could a man go on loving a woman when he believed she hated him?

He examined Sara closely. She was so comely, he'd do anything for her. How could it be true, that Will had stopped loving her? But how could a woman love a man who she believed hated her?

"Will's not right to treat you this way," James said.

"No one can blame him," Sara said, "with me in this condition." He knew she meant her broken hip. "Now you run along, Jamie. You don't want to be left behind when the men go."

He looked to the bank and saw that the men were driving the animals away. The rafts would be casting off any minute. He had yet to say good-bye to

Cady and Mrs. Walker. He scanned the crowded rafts for them.

"Jamie!" his pa called from shore. He was on Mackie, driving the oxen up the bank.

Jeremy was next to him, on Corncob. "Fetch Bolt and come along!" his brother shouted.

James had tied Bolt to a fence post near the dock. No longer having a wagon to lie under, Scraps had placed herself in Bolt's shadow, where she was enjoying the cool. Bolt was calmly nibbling at some grass, awaiting James's return.

Will, on Tempest, was just disappearing over the ridge of the bank. The other men had already left, retracing their steps eastward on the trail. In a few miles, they'd reach the fork to the Barlow Road, and head south.

Then James spotted Mrs. Walker six rafts away. She was peering around as if she'd lost something in the confusion.

James started to hail her, but thought better of it. There was no time for farewells. Where had Cady gone to? James wondered. She must be here somewhere. Well, there was no time to say good-bye to her now. Wherever she was. And anyway, he'd see her in a week.

He leaped onto shore and ran to Bolt. For the first time that day, he felt weary. He'd been dashing around, lifting, and pushing since daybreak. Now he was bone tired.

He unhitched Bolt and climbed on his back. James wasn't keen on riding Bolt too often—he was still a growing horse, and had to be treated carefully. But right now James couldn't take another step.

"Yah," he said. Bolt trotted up the bank to catch up with the other men, Scraps skipping along beside them. James didn't even turn around to catch a last glimpse of the women.

James tried not to trip over his own feet as Bolt stepped gaily next to him. It was a lesson well learned, what his pa had told him about pacing himself. Of course, Pa had also told him to go ahead and work off his excitement. Now he was paying for it.

He was worn down and footsore, tuckered and drooping. He was walking now because earlier, when riding Bolt, he'd dozed in the saddle. On the whole, it was safer to keep himself awake by stumbling along on his own feet than to risk falling off his horse.

James was lagging behind the rest of the men. At the end of their first day on the Barlow Road, the men would camp some two thousand feet up. The trail meandered through several canyons and over a number of buttes, so the total climb was much more. James realized it was not something to be done after a morning spent knocking himself out.

Ahead of him Pa and Jeremy herded the oxen along the trail. Without their heavy yokes and a wagon to pull, the oxen were much livelier. For the first time in months, Pa had to worry about them bolting.

As James trudged along, he thought about the adventures he'd had. Seeing a man shot in Independence, Missouri, and another one hanged for it at Fort Laramie. Catching a trio of desperadoes along Sublette's Cutoff. Finding Scraps in a magical wood in the Rocky Mountains. Saving Bolt from mean old Mr. Meacham.

He wondered what had happened to Mr. Meacham and his wife after they left the train. Colonel Stewart had warned them not to go. James wondered if he'd ever find out whether Mr. Meacham made it to California alive.

Bolt snorted, and James slapped him on the flank affectionately. Bolt was much stronger and heavier than he had been when James acquired him. James looked at Scraps, bounding down the trail ahead of them. The little dog was healthier and fatter too.

Then a memory came to James—something he hadn't thought of in a long time. The day before the train set out, he and his pa had bought some supplies at a general store in Independence. What was the name of the place? P. Whitfield, Provisioner, that was it.

James had stepped onto the big feed scale, to see how much he weighed. He was a pound short of one hundred, so Pa had filled his pocket with shot to make it an even hundred.

James smiled at the memory. He wondered if, like Bolt and Scraps, he had gained any weight during the journey. He didn't feel any bigger, though sometimes his clothes tugged on him a little. But these things were hard to tell.

Suddenly he became aware of a rustle in the leaves behind him. The trail here was lined with firs and pines—not a thick forest, but enough cover to hide a bear.

Scraps barked loudly, and raced off the trail and behind a nearby tree. James waited nervously while Scraps rooted around in the bushes. Maybe it had been nothing more than a squirrel rustling those leaves.

After a few seconds Scraps came bounding out of the bushes, wagging her tail happily.

Not a bear, James thought. *Must have been a squirrel after all*. He looked up the trail. Pa and Jeremy were now several hundred feet in front of him.

Jeremy turned, an impatient look on his face. "Hurry up, Jamie!" he yelled.

And from the bushes where Scraps had been nosing around came a voice: "Yeah. Hurry up, snail boy."

James spun toward the bushes. He'd know that voice anywhere.

It was Cady's.

TWELVE

DEVIL'S HALF ACRE

Colonel Stewart and Pierre Delaroux stood with their fists on their hips, shaking their heads.

"The other women are long gone by now, I expect," the colonel said bitterly. "Anyway, it's twelve miles back down the trail." He took off his big hat and ran his fingers through his long golden hair. "What the devil are we going to do with you?" he asked Cady for the fourth time.

Cady crossed her arms, raised her chin defiantly, and refused to answer. She was trying to tough it out, but James could tell she was worried. She probably hadn't expected everyone to be so angry with her.

"Cady," Mr. Walker said sternly, "why did you sneak off like that?"

"That old raft ride wasn't going to be nearly as exciting as blazing the trail round Mount Hood with the menfolk," she muttered. "I couldn't let James have all the fun."

James rolled his eyes. Sometimes Cady's competitiveness went too far.

"All the fun!" Mr. Walker exploded. "We're not playing games here! You should know that by now. Cady, this is about the most foolish, inconsiderate, reckless stunt you've ever pulled!"

James didn't think he'd ever seen Cady's pa so angry. Usually he was quite slow to scold Cady, even when she deserved it. Now he was really letting her have it.

"We're heading for high mountain territory," Mr. Walker said. "The way the weather's been lately, we might be facing snow. I wasn't planning on having to look after my foolheaded daughter. And what about your mother, missing you on the raft? She must be worried sick by now."

Cady hung her head. "I'm sorry, Father. I didn't mean to cause any pain. I wasn't thinking. I know you'll never be able to forgive me."

James rolled his eyes again. She was really laying it on thick.

"I'm no good," Cady went on. "You oughta just chuck me by the side of the trail and move on."

Mr. Walker looked at Cady for a long while. Then, in a calmer voice, he asked, "How did you get away without your mother knowing it?"

"I told her I'd be riding on Mrs. Gregg's raft for a

100

piece." She was trying to hide it, but James could tell Cady was pleased with herself. "I reckoned that in all the bedlam Mother wouldn't know I wasn't there until hours after. Maybe not even until tonight."

James's pa spoke up. "Well, since no one from the ferry landing came after us to ask about her, Cady's plan must have worked. By the time the women know she's missing, it'll be too late for them to turn back. We seem to have no choice in the matter."

James couldn't believe it. Was Cady actually going to be allowed to come with the men?

Colonel Stewart and Pierre Delaroux shook their heads some more. Both of them were running their hands through their hair.

"What are we going to do with you?" Delaroux asked this time, more in resignation than in anger.

Cady blinked at him and smiled brightly. "Why, take me along, I expect."

For the next two days, James hardly spoke to Cady. He was mad at her for tagging along. But he was even angrier that, once the decision had been made to take her along, none of the other men seemed mad at her any longer. Even Colonel Stewart and Pierre Delaroux stopped shaking their heads.

Well, James wasn't that quick to forgive.

On top of everything else, when he asked his pa if he could take Bolt hunting one morning, Pa said yes, on one condition: that he take Cady with him.

101

Pa wanted them to be friends again. And besides, Cady still needed to learn how to take care of herself in the wilderness. So it was either take Cady with him, or not go hunting at all. Reluctantly James agreed to take her.

But no one could make him be nice about it.

James trotted Bolt along the narrow stony path that led away from the Barlow Road. James supposed it was an Indian trail. A loaded rifle lay across his lap, barrel pointed upward so as not to lose the bullet.

"Why do you get to ride while I'm walking?" Cady asked him sharply.

"Because Bolt's my horse, not yours," he answered. "Besides, I told you I didn't want you along on this hunt. You're just going to scare off the game."

"I didn't last time," she argued.

"No, but you didn't manage to hit anything, either," James replied. "And there were jackrabbits everywhere."

"That was my first hunt." Cady sniffed. "I'm sure I'm a better shot now. Anyway, your pa said I could come."

"And that's the only reason I'm letting you stay with me," James muttered testily. "Now hurry up, you're walking too slow."

"I'm going as fast as I can," Cady said. "The air's so thin, it's hard to get a good breath."

They were crossing Devil's Half Acre, a treacherous pass almost a mile up in the Cascade Range. Even Bolt was breathing heavily.

James sucked in as much cold clean air as he could. It smelled of pine sap and fir needles. All around him the giant trees sprang out of the rocky floor. The scrub brush below them was twisted into fantastic shapes by the wind.

He'd never seen anything like Devil's Half Acre—the huge pine cones scattered among the boulders, the immense jagged stumps of trees that had fallen over with age. It was nothing like the soft misty valley back in Pennsylvania where he'd grown up.

James knew he had to put the past behind him. He was in Oregon now—Oregon City itself was less than fifty miles away. And despite the strangeness of the land, already it was feeling like home.

"Slow down, James!" Cady called.

He turned Bolt around. Cady lagged behind him by a good fifty feet now. She plodded heavily up the trail, her shoulders slouched, her chest heaving.

"Deer aren't going to wait all day for us!" he yelled gleefully. "Get a move on, tortoise girl."

"I'm coming, I'm coming!" Cady hollered. "If you think I'm going so slow, why don't you walk for a while?"

"'Cause I'm smart enough to be riding a horse!" James shouted back. He dropped Bolt's reins and crossed his arms impatiently. The rifle was balanced across the horn of his saddle.

Suddenly he felt Bolt stiffen beneath him. The horse's ears flattened against his skull. Something was wrong.

"James!" Cady yelled. "There's a—"

Her cry was cut off by a piercing scream.

Bolt started. It was all James could do to grab the reins with one hand and wheel the horse around.

James's heart raced as he turned to see what had made the terrifying cry. . . . Above him, not ten feet away, a snarling panther crouched on a rocky ledge.

James stared into the big yellow eyes of the angry cat, and swallowed hard.

It raised its heavy whiskered lips over its long white fangs and hissed. The muscles in its shoulders were bunched and ready to spring. Its golden tail twitched rhythmically.

James fumbled for the rifle, then realized it had fallen off his lap when he'd spun around.

The panther howled again, chilling James to the bone.

Bolt reared, and James grabbed on to his mane to keep from being thrown. He patted Bolt's neck and made shushing noises to soothe him. The panther was sure to spring at any sudden movement. But without the rifle, James was defenseless against the big cat. All he and Bolt could do was hope for mercy.

He glanced back at Cady. She was frozen in her tracks just twenty feet away.

"Run, Cady!" he shouted. "Run!"

The panther let out another piercing scream. To James it seemed as if all the devils in the underworld had made their way to this one little half acre in the Cascades.

Cady remained stock still.

"Cady, run!" he urged.

The hairs on the back of his neck stood on end as the panther growled lowly.

"Now!"

Cady met his eye and held it for an instant. She winked coolly.

Then she darted for the gun.

James spun around to face the panther in time to see it spring from the ledge.

In that instant James knew he was a goner.

He could see the unsheathed claws slashing down toward him, the sharp fangs set in the blood-red gums, the strange, unearthly yellow eyes.

James braced himself for the death blow, and then—
Crack!

The panther writhed violently in midair, screaming. No longer intent on its prey, the cat twisted and turned, the arc of its leap carrying it forward. It crashed into James, knocking him off Bolt.

He fell heavily, his head striking the gravelly

ground. For several seconds he lay on his left side, motionless, trying to regain his senses. Then he opened his eyes.

Next to him lay the massive head of the panther, yellow eyes rolled up into its skull, bright pink tongue showing between its long teeth.

James blinked slowly and groaned.

Then Cady put her boot on his right shoulder and rolled him over onto his back.

She looked down at him with an expression of infinite satisfaction. "Who says I can't shoot?" she asked. "Killed that panther with one bullet."

THIRTEEN

CAUGHT IN BARLOW PASS

C ady lorded it over James unmercifully all of that day.

"Now we're even," she kept saying. "You saved my life at the South Platte, and I saved yours at Devil's Half Acre. You'd have been torn to pieces by that panther if it weren't for me and my skill with a gun."

James nodded stoically. He supposed Cady had a right to gloat after all the times he'd reminded her of how she couldn't swim. And he had to admit it *had* been a right good shot—above the clavicle and straight through the heart.

They'd had a hard time settling Bolt after the cat was dead. Any horse would be spooked by a panther. Finally James and Cady had loaded the cat onto Bolt's back and returned to camp.

The men were impressed, to say the least. And

even more so when they were told who'd shot the panther.

"Why, Cady," James's pa said, "I certainly am glad you stowed away with us. If it weren't for you, Jamie would have been panther victuals."

"I can't say I'm not still angry at you," Mr. Walker added, "but this does ease the feeling somewhat."

"Shall we call you Artemis, goddess of the moon and of hunting in Greek myth?" Lord Callanbridge teased. "Or perhaps the Roman goddess of the hunt, Diana?"

"'Cady' is just fine," she said, blushing.

James sighed to himself as Cady basked shamelessly in the praise and congratulations.

Then Pierre Delaroux stepped up. "The panther you have shot, she is a fine animal. We butcher her tonight, and tomorrow I begin, eh, how do you say, confecting?"

"Fashioning," Colonel Stewart corrected him.

"Yes, fashioning a cape from the pelt," Delaroux finished. "You would fancy that, yes?"

Cady's eyes grew round as saucers, and her mouth dropped open. "Land's sakes alive, I sure would, Mr. Delaroux. Can you make it with the mouth wide open and the fangs bared, that I could wear on my head like a bonnet, and the claws still on and everything?"

The big trapper laughed loudly. "I will try, I will try to do as you request."

Within the hour Delaroux had skinned the beast and cleaned the pelt. The next morning he pounded it with the rocks, softening it enough for Cady to wear.

Despite Cady's request, Delaroux had removed the teeth, along with skin of the entire lower jaw. The upper lip of the cat sort of draped across Cady's forehead, the cat's ears flapping down the back of her neck. Delaroux had laced a leather strap at the base of the cat's head, which Cady could tie around her neck to keep the skin from sliding off.

With it on, Cady looked like a savage beast herself, a wild girl of the untamed wilderness. The effect was undeniably dramatic.

James almost told her he wished he had one. Instead he informed her that her new cape was a tad fresh smelling.

Cady replied that now she really fit right in with the menfolk.

All morning she wore it, making howling noises and pretending to leap at James. His patience was wearing thin, but he tried to look on the bright side—Cady's competitiveness was cured, at least for the time being. And on the whole, she was a lot more fun to be around when she wasn't trying to beat him at something.

It was almost—almost—worth getting attacked by a panther to keep her happy, he told himself.

Throughout the morning the snow-clad summit of Mount Hood drifted in and out of thick white clouds. Now, when it was less than five miles away, it was completely obscured.

The men, and Cady of course, were hiking through Barlow Pass. They were nearly a mile up in the Cascades, and the ground was covered with a crusty frost. James knew this wasn't like the frost they'd often seen in the high elevations. It was thicker and more brittle, and it wasn't burning off with the day's sun.

In fact, the day was quite chilly—near freezing, and getting colder by the hour.

James now wished he had a panther-skin cloak for two reasons: first, to make him look like a wild animal, and second, to keep him warm.

Ahead of him he saw the tawny hide of the big cat draped over Cady's form. She was prancing along the trail, still ever so pleased with herself and her new garment.

"I swan," James muttered. "Sometimes that girl's nothing but a nettle in my side."

"Oh, she's a pest and a bother," Jeremy agreed.

James turned, startled. He hadn't meant for his brother to overhear his complaint.

"But count yourself lucky to be so plagued," Jeremy continued. "Missy and I, we fought like cats and dogs. Why, one day I got so angry with her, I had to throw myself into Benson's Creek to cool down."

"Is this going to turn into another Missy story?" James asked rudely.

"No," Jeremy replied. "What I'm trying to say is, there's not a day goes by, not an hour, that I don't think of Missy and wish she were here by my side, if only to nettle me. Cady's a fine girl and you know it, and you should treat her well now, while you have the chance. Because when we get to Oregon City, she's going with her family, and you're going with ours. And you may never see her again."

Jeremy strode ahead rapidly, turning only to add, "And someday you may rue not valuing what you're now so quick to scorn."

James tried vainly to think of a smart reply. But he knew Jeremy was right. His brother might not know much, but he did know about missing people.

And it had never before occurred to James that in less than a week he might have to say good-bye, permanently, to Cady.

He stood and watched the men drive the animals up the trail, as snow commenced sprinkling the toes of his boots.

The snow fell, lightly at first and then harder, spiraling down in sparkly white whirlwinds that scattered and became icy biting gusts. The gusts came one after another, closer and closer together, piling on top, till the wind became one screaming unbroken howl.

Large, fluffy feathers at the beginning, the flakes of snow were now small rock-hard pellets of ice.

Whipped by the wind, they stung the faces and hands of the travelers. James was reminded of the six-day dust storm the train had endured back on the Platte. This storm was just as blinding, just as painful, just as debilitating.

And it was cold, besides.

Once the gusts came, the men ceased attempting to drive the animals and made camp for the night. Even had the men tried to go forward, the animals would have refused. They were wise enough not to attempt travel along a rocky mountain path in a blinding snowstorm.

With most of their possessions packed away on the rafts with the women, the men huddled in skimpy tents and supped on rations of dry hardtack.

The wind wouldn't allow for a fire, so the men slept together in twos and threes for the warmth. There were only fourteen people in the train now: Colonel Stewart and Pierre Delaroux; Mr. Jennington and Mr. Teague; Will Gantry and Lord Callanbridge; Mr. Walker and Cady; Mr. Smoot, Mr. Connell, and Mr. Sundstrom; and the three Greggs.

After dinner, James asked Pa if he could go visit with Cady and Mr. Walker. He was still feeling bad about what Jeremy had said to him earlier in the day.

"It's too dangerous out there, son," Pa said. "But if you're worried, I'll go see that they're safe."

James nodded. He noticed Jeremy giving him an

approving look now that he was expressing some concern for Cady.

Pa returned and reported that she was bundled snugly in her warm panther cape. In the tent next to her, he said, Mr. Walker was making due with a wool blanket.

James was pleased to note Jeremy shuddering in envy at those glad tidings.

As night fell cold, wet, windy, and miserable, James considered their plight. Who knew how long this storm would last? If the snow got too high, they'd have trouble getting out of Barlow's Pass at all. They might be stuck here for the winter. Better not to think about that, James decided.

He shivered as he scooted closer between his pa and Jeremy. At least one thing about this storm was an improvement on the dust storm on the plains. In the earlier storm, water was scarce, and your mouth and throat parched painfully. In this storm, there was no shortage of drinkables.

All you had to do was reach your hand out of the tent and scoop some up.

FOURTEEN

OVER THE RUGGED MOUNTAIN

It snowed through the night and all the next day, too, fierce and blindingly, and unutterably cold.

Breakfast was dried johnnycake and melted snow. James, Jeremy, and Pa, along with Scraps, sat quietly in the tent. Pa brought out a small block of wood and a knife. He'd been carving the block for weeks, ever since he'd picked it up in the Black Hills of the Rockies.

It was going to be a box for holding Ma's thimbles and needles. The outside was decorated with an elaborate composition of tiny birds, flowers, leaves, and insects. The hinges that held the lid to the base were made entirely out of wood, in a clever design that Pa had invented himself.

As Pa carved into the block, the unmistakable odor of cut wood was released into the small space of the tent.

"Smells like summer," James commented. It was

strange to think, in the middle of a raging snowstorm, that little more than a month ago they'd been traveling across the blistery hot plain of the Snake River.

"Funny you should say that," Pa replied, not taking his eyes off his work. "Cut wood always smells of summer to me, too."

James smiled. He liked to think he and his pa thought the same way.

"You fellows know what kind of wood this is?" Pa asked conversationally.

Without bark or leaves as clues, James had no idea what the wood might be. "I couldn't say," he admitted.

"By the look of the grain, I'd guess cottonwood," Jeremy ventured.

"You're close," Pa said, pleased. "Cottonwood's a kind of poplar, and so's this wood. But this is *balsam* poplar. It's also called tacamahac, by the Spanish."

Pa shifted in the cramped tent and held the block out to Jeremy. "Take a good whiff of that," he said.

Jeremy did so, then handed it to James.

"Smells spicy," James said. "Minty."

"You know what else they call this wood?" Pa asked. The boys shook their heads.

"Balm of Gilead," Pa said. "Like in the Bible. I reckon it's not the same wood as grows in Palestine, but the smell is similar, or folks imagined it was."

Pa pressed the block against his thick brown mustache and inhaled heartily. "The Israelites made

116

healing ointments from balsamic resins. How does the verse go? 'Is there no balm in Gilead?' Here, James." He dug into his small knapsack and got out his battered old Bible. "Look up the passage for us. It's Jeremiah, I believe."

James flipped through the Bible to Jeremiah and found the spot. "Jeremiah, chapter eight," he said. "Verse twenty-two: 'Is there no balm in Gilead; is there no physician there? Why then is not the health of the daughter of my people recovered?'"

"That's the one," Pa said with satisfaction.

James read through Jeremiah some more. It reminded him of the way Mrs. Walker used to be before Scott died—full of fearful upbraidings and exhortations to repent.

James preferred Bible stories with heroes in them: Daniel in the lion's den, David and Goliath, even Moses in the bulrushes. Secretly, though, he thought none of them measured up to *Ivanhoe*, which he'd read four times.

He turned to the front of the Bible and read the inscription on the first page:

> *Samuel J. Gregg's Bible*
> *O holy Bible, book divine,*
> *Precious treasure, thou art mine.*
> *April 17th, 1824*

James did some quick arithmetic. His pa had

been the same age, twelve, when he'd received this Bible as James was now. James wondered for a moment if his pa had liked the same parts of the Bible that he did. He probably had. After all, they were a lot alike.

James, Pa, and Jeremy huddled together in the little canvas tent for the rest of the day. Only once did Pa go outside, to see about the animals and to make certain the Walkers were safe. He reported that the oxen were stoically abiding the storm as only oxen could, and that the horses looked all right too.

The wind blew, and the snow piled up against the tent. By late afternoon, the snow was over a foot and a half deep. Inside the tent the air was stuffy and wet, and uncomfortably chilly. James wanted one of those panther-skin cloaks more than ever.

And dinner was melted snow and hardtack.

Pa said that if the storm didn't end soon, they might have to slaughter one of the oxen.

"They can't last forever in this weather," he explained. "We can certainly use the meat, and if it comes to it, we can use the carcass for shelter."

James didn't relish sleeping in the body of a dead ox, even if it was warm. As he lay next to his pa and his brother that night, he recalled some words from Jeremiah. They had come before the part about no balm in Gilead, and they did not bode well for the party of men: "The harvest is past, the summer is ended, and we are not saved."

118

* * *

Breakfast the following morning was, for a change, melted snow with johnnycake *and* hardtack. The wind whistled and piped, and the snow piled higher and higher.

James asked Pa if he could go outside for a moment to see how Bolt was doing.

"I'll let you go," Pa said. "But don't wander off. It's easy to get lost in a storm like this, and I'd never be able to find you."

Bolt stood in snow up to his hocks, head bowed low, his nose only inches above the level of the rising snow. His eyelashes were crusted with ice, and James brushed them open with his fingers. Bolt whinnied gratefully when James fed him a johnnycake—not normal food for a horse, but the circumstances were extraordinary. Scraps had been living off it for the last day and a half.

Before returning to the tent, James visited Corncob and Mackie and gave them a little johnnycake too.

"Bolt's not doing well," James told Pa when he got back to the tent. "I don't know how much longer he'll last. And the other horses are no better, maybe worse." Corncob had barely had the strength to chew the johnnycake.

"I know it, Jamie," Pa said. "We're in a pretty pickle. If the storm doesn't end soon, we'll lose the animals. We need to get moving, regardless of the conditions. If we stay here much longer, it'll be to dig our own graves."

James sensed that his pa was coming to some sort of conclusion.

"I'll go talk to Mr. Delaroux and the colonel," Pa said, wrapping his coat around himself. "Find out what they advise."

James, Jeremy, and Scraps sat in the tent and listened to the wind howl outside. There was nothing any of them could do other than await Pa's word from the colonel.

Nearly two hours passed. James became concerned that Pa had got lost in the storm. He was relieved when Pa finally burst through the tent flap, his mustache and beard caked with snow.

"Colonel says we're moving out in the morning," he gasped. "Whether the storm abates or not."

James swallowed hard. Trekking through knee-deep snow was only marginally preferable to sitting helpless in a tent.

"What took you so long, Pa?" Jeremy asked.

"I dropped in on the Walkers," he said. "They're fine—no worse'n us, anyway. Then I said howdy to Harlan Teague and Henry Jennington, then to Lord Callanbridge and Will. They're uncomfortable too, but alive enough." He paused.

"And . . ." Jeremy prompted. "I know you weren't paying social calls for two hours. What happened with the colonel and Pierre Delaroux?"

120

Pa got out his hickory comb, and commenced removing the ice from his beard. "Well, Colonel Stewart and Mr. Delaroux weren't convinced it was better to move on," he said slowly. "I reasoned with them, but they didn't see my point of view. So I reasoned with them some more." Pa smiled to himself as he tugged on his beard. "And then they did."

James couldn't imagine what Pa could have said to make the likes of the colonel and Pierre Delaroux change their minds. They were such stalwart, unwavering men.

But he knew that when Pa was convinced he was right, there wasn't a soul alive who could stand up to him.

Not even a stern military man and a big French trapper.

After a quick breakfast of melted snow and hardtack, James and the other men broke camp. The wind was not as strong this morning, and the snow was coming down as flakes rather than as pellets. The men took this as a good sign. At least it wasn't as painful to the skin to walk through.

James rounded up the horses while Jeremy prepared the oxen. Pa moved from group to group, checking to see that everyone was ready. Mr. Connell's feet had been numb since the previous morning, and he feared frostbite. But he was eager to move out.

Under better conditions, the way out of Barlow Pass and down the mountains would have posed few problems. Oregon City was little more than forty miles away—three days, four at the most.

The snow blotted out the trail, however, and made navigating tricky. Numerous times the colonel led the men down gullies or up slopes, only to encounter impassable obstacles. Doubling back, retracing their steps often, the men made slow progress.

Plodding along next to Bolt, James doubted they made any progress at all. He wondered if the colonel and Mr. Delaroux might not have been right in preferring to wait out the storm. On the other hand, James was less cold now that he was walking.

At one point during the day he trotted up next to Cady to see how she was doing. The ears of her panther-skin hood were piled high with snow.

"Wish I had me one of those panther coats," James said.

"It's a cape, not a coat," Cady corrected him. "And if I had another, I'd give it to you, you know I would," she added generously.

"I'm taking you up on that next time you shoot a panther," James said.

Cady smiled. "You believe we'll get out of this alive?"

"Alive?" James repeated. "Why, of course we will. We can't come all this way only to die on

Oregon City's doorstep." He tried to sound sure of himself, for her sake.

"I want you to know, James." Cady's voice went serious. "If we don't make it, I'm still glad I ran off with the men. No place I'd rather die than with you."

"Aww . . ." James slapped her with his hat, knocking the snow off her panther ears. "Same goes for me, I reckon," he said honestly. Then he ran back to walk with Pa and Jeremy.

Hour after hour he lifted one foot and placed it in the deep footprint in front of him, then lifted the other, and so on. On and on.

And still the snow fell.

The men didn't stop moving until nightfall came, then made camp quickly in the dark. It had been an exhausting day, but there were signs of hope. Once or twice the rising moon had peeked out from behind the clouds. None of the animals had collapsed, though several horses, including Corncob, were breathing poorly in the thin air. And the feeling had returned to Mr. Connell's feet.

At sunup the men moved on. The snow was lighter now, only a sprinkling, but the way was as confusing as ever.

Backtracking, facing about, turning around, circling back, the men walked dutifully on. Colonel Stewart's and Pierre Delaroux's senses of direction were tested to the limit. And still James could have sworn he'd seen the same pine tree four times.

Finally James gave up on looking around him and simply followed the footprints without raising his eyes. He was cold and tired. Tired after more than five months on the trail, tired after two days' wallowing through knee-deep snow. Cold in every extremity, cold down in the core of his belly. Hungry, too.

So he followed the footsteps, not looking up, hour after hour, mile after mile. Counting them at first, left, right, one, two, losing count somewhere in the three thousands. Never looking up, stepping forward, lost in a dream of walking over the rugged mountain and through the piled snow.

Then a sound broke the daze he'd fallen into. The sound of a bird calling. He knew the call—the fluting, piping notes of a bluebird, just as he used to hear them through the window of a little house in a valley in Pennsylvania.

But bluebirds don't call in a snowstorm.

James looked up. The trees held only a dusting of snow. The bright yellow sun shone in a sky bluer than any blue he'd ever seen before.

He looked down. Without his being aware of it, the footprints he'd been following had become shallower and shallower. The next one was only an inch or so deep.

They were down from the mountaintop.

FIFTEEN

TRAIL'S END

The way into Oregon City was simple once the last pass of the Cascades was gained. The men walked the final twenty miles, through a tall timber forest, in a buzz of excitement. The animals sensed that the end of the trail was near, and they stepped with renewed vigor. Even old Corncob regained the spring in his step.

It was only in the last mile or so that Cady slowed down.

"Why are you dragging your feet, girl?" James asked her. "Don't you know we're almost there?"

They could see the smoke from the chimneys of Oregon City rising in the sky to the west.

"I'm in no hurry," Cady said.

"No hurry?" James was astonished. "Aren't you dying to see your—" Then it hit him. "Oh. I expect your ma's going to be angry with you for running off, huh?"

"Angry's not the half of it. Mother's going to tan my hide." Cady shook her head. The ears of her panther skin flopped back and forth forlornly. "Oh, why don't I ever think about the consequences before I go ahead and do a thing?"

James couldn't answer that one. He had noticed that Cady was a mite impulsive. That's what made her so much fun, though.

"Maybe I could help you," he offered. "We could tell her it was my idea—that I dared you to run off."

"Thanks, James, but it'll never work. Father knows you had nothing to do with it, and he's sure to tell Mother." Cady sighed long and loud. "I'll just have to answer to her myself."

Soon afterward the men drove the animals into a broad field outside of Oregon City, where dozens of tents were pitched around an equal number of wagons. It wasn't long before Pierre Delaroux managed to locate the women and children of the Stewart train.

James and Jeremy raced to greet their ma and Elizabeth.

"Am I glad to see you!" Ma shouted, hugging James, who'd reached her first, and then Jeremy, who'd been cut off by Elizabeth. "We were so worried you'd gotten caught in the mountain—we've been camped here for two days waiting."

James and Jeremy talked over each other to tell Ma and Elizabeth the exciting story of how they'd trekked through the mountain snows.

Then Pa came up, wrapping Elizabeth in one arm and Ma in the other. He gave her a big long hug and kiss.

"Boys, boys!" Ma hollered when Pa let her up for air. "Settle down. And that means you too, Samuel."

Pa grinned bashfully, pleased at being scolded so by his wife.

"I want to hear all the details of your adventure," Ma said. "But first I have to know, was Cady with you?"

James nodded quickly. "Yes, ma'am."

"Thank the Lord," Ma said. "And she's well too?"

James nodded again. "She saved my life. Shot herself a panther."

"Have mercy, a panther!" Ma exclaimed. "You young'uns will be the end of me yet. Wolves, snakes, panthers! It's a wonder you didn't wind up wrestling a bear, like old Alonzo Tanner."

James and Jeremy laughed, and Ma hugged them again.

"Well, I surely am glad Cady's safe," she said, shaking her head grimly. "Maybe Mrs. Walker's condition will improve some when she hears the good news."

"She's ailing?" James asked.

"Big with child she is, Jamie," Ma said. "And not having an easy time of it."

Having grown up on a farm, James knew the seriousness of a troubled pregnancy. Three years ago their mare Dancer had birthed a stillborn foal, and herself died not two hours later.

"When we came to the portage at the Cascades," Ma continued, "Mrs. Walker was too weak to walk, much less carry any of her belongings. All of us had to hire men to help tote the wagons. But she had to be carried bodily to the lower rafts. She's awfully weak, the poor dear."

James wondered briefly how Cady's reunion with her ma was going. If Mrs. Walker was feeling poorly, at least she couldn't tan Cady's hide.

Jeremy asked Ma what the raft trip had been like.

"Oh, the Columbia's a glorious fine river," she said. "The canyon walls drop down hundreds of feet in places. It was something like the Snake, only this time I was looking up at the gorge instead of down at the river."

"I'd like to see it sometime," said James.

"After all the rivers and gorges you've seen," Ma said, smiling, "I'd think you'd find Fort Vancouver more interesting. We stopped there, to catch rafts up the Willamette. It's nothing like Fort Boise, or those other filthy sties."

James knew his ma had never much approved of the goings-on at western outposts.

"Fort Vancouver is wonderful," she went on. "Why, outside the fort is a fine new sawmill, and orchards full of apples, peaches, pears, plums—every fruit you can name. Grapes, melons, strawberries.

Figs as big as prairie hailstones. Beans and peas piled high in the marketplace, tomatoes, cabbages, cucumbers. And Samuel—" She turned to Pa. "You wouldn't believe it. The beautiful wheat and oats, barley and potatoes."

"And six hundred and forty acres of fertile, abundant, bounteous Oregon soil is mine for the claiming and clearing," Pa said, laughing heartily.

James was laughing too. It was a joyous laughter of pure giddiness, for he was happy beyond words to learn that Oregon was all it was promised to be.

"I know Mr. Delaroux would like Fort Vancouver," Ma continued. "I heard nothing but French the entire time I was there. Oh, and Jeremy!"

"Yes, ma'am," Jeremy said.

"You'll never guess what I saw."

What else was there she could have seen? James asked himself.

"Ships!" she said. "Ships in the harbor. From New York and Baltimore, and London, and one from the Sandwich Islands. Imagine that—all the way from Oahu, halfway across the Pacific!"

"Sailing for San Francisco, I don't doubt," said Jeremy, grinning, "taking on fortune seekers from Oregon as cargo."

Suddenly the merriment drained out of the Greggs, as Jeremy's words sank in. Fortune seekers from Oregon, on their way to San Francisco.

To hunt for gold, James added silently, sullenly.

It didn't seem fair, he thought. Here they were, together at last in Oregon City, the destination they'd dreamed of these many months.

And his brother now eager to abandon them.

After settling back into the tent and wagon, feeding and watering the horses, and resting a spot, Pa invited James to accompany him to town.

"Town?" James asked.

"Why, yes," Pa responded. "Oregon City's just half a mile down the road there." He gestured toward the horizon, and once again James noticed smoke trailing into the air.

It had been a long time since James had seen a human encampment more substantial than a trappers' fort. He'd almost forgotten what a town looked like.

"Sure, I'll go with you, Pa," he said.

"Good. Saddle up Bolt and let's get a move on. Mackie's raring to see the big city."

As they rode the short distance into Oregon City, James recalled going to Independence, Missouri, with his pa and his brother back in May. He'd ridden in the wagon then, not on his own horse. James smiled at the thought of how young he'd been, how little of the world he'd seen.

Now, as he sat astride his own horse, he felt he was almost grown up. He'd helped his family cross a continent. He'd seen more sights than most men three times his age. He'd experienced a whole world along the Oregon Trail. And much of that world, he knew, was fading into the past, never to come again.

On the outskirts of town, James spotted some elderly Flatheads. Like those old Indians, whose ways were disappearing, the farmers and homesteaders who'd followed the trail would soon be overwhelmed. The farther west James had got, the more talk he'd heard of California. And gold.

Rather than clear land, plant crops, and harvest riches out of the ground by honest labor, fortune seekers wanted to make their fortunes the easy way—by picking it up off the ground in the form of gold nuggets.

There was something dishonorable in gaining wealth that way, James concluded as he and Pa rode up the main street of Oregon City.

It wasn't exactly a big city. In fact, it was smaller than Independence, Missouri. But it was a fine, clean, prosperous little settlement of mostly one- and two-story wood-shingled buildings.

Businesses catering to new settlers crowded one on top of another. James counted a feed store, a gunsmith, a wheelwright, a cobbler, a dressmaker. Even a silversmith.

James had wondered if there would be enough commerce in Oregon City to support the hardware store Mr. Walker planned on opening. By the look of the busy street and thriving shops, James was satisfied Mr. Walker's venture would be a success.

Then he noticed a trading post with a large scale for weighing sacks of grain displayed prominently in the window. "Pa," he called.

"Yes, son?"

"Remember Mr. Whitfield's store in Independence?"

Pa scratched his beard. "Where we bought the flour and shot? I reckon I do."

"Remember how I weighed just short of a hundred pounds? Maybe I'd like to stand on the scales again." James nodded at the trading post.

"Maybe you would, would you?" Pa asked. "Well, then, let's see how much you've grown."

They tied their horses to a hitching post in front of the store, then entered. The room was piled high with things folks had dragged two thousand miles on the trail, only to trade away in Oregon City. Dressers, beds, mirrors, hatboxes, carved picture frames with real oil paintings in them, glass plates, clocks, and countless other items were piled everywhere.

In the back of the room a half-dozen men lounged, playing cards and checkers, chatting sleepily in the cool and dark. James got the feeling these fellows could be found there any time of the day, any day of the week.

James and Pa made their way to the scale. "Go ahead, son," Pa said.

James stepped onto the springy metal base of the

scale. Above him, the needle whirled a third of the way around the scale's large round face, bounced back and forth for a few seconds, and came to a rest.

James looked up. The needle pointed to one hundred and eight pounds.

"Nine pounds in less than six months," said Pa. "That's mighty impressive. And you don't even have any shot in your pockets."

Laughing, James scanned the room. It certainly was a crowded store. Then his eye fell on something curious.

Silently he stepped off the scale and approached a pile of clothing. A man's maroon velvet vest. Bright green breeches. Long coat and tartan cravat. They were unlike any attire he'd ever seen.

Except on one man.

James searched through the clothes and discovered a large white handkerchief. Sure enough, embroidered in fancy lettering in a corner were the initials A.D.B.

Almaris Drummond Belvoir.

Lord Callanbridge.

These were the clothes that had been stolen from the lord! And there, in the corner, were some wooden boxes with glass lids. James rushed over and looked inside. Lord Callanbridge's bird collection! Would he be glad to hear about this.

James called his pa over and told him what he'd discovered. They were discussing the find when one of the men from the back of the store ambled over.

"Our friend'll be awful happy to have his belongings back," James said to the man. "He doesn't have a cent to his name."

"He'll have a hard time buying them, then," the man replied.

"*Buying* them!" James said, shocked. "Why, they're his already. They were stolen from him."

"That's as may be," said the man. "But I traded a jug of good corn liquor for these clothes, and they're mine until someone makes me a suitable offer."

"The man has a point, Jamie," Pa said calmly. "He couldn't have known the things were stolen. We can't ask him to take Lord Callanbridge's loss."

The man nodded. "Eugene Grant's the name." He extended his hand, and Pa shook it. So did James, reluctantly.

"Samuel Gregg, and this here's my son James," Pa said. "We've just come in on the Stewart train."

"Well, now, the Stewart train," said Mr. Grant. "I just heard tell of some folks that split off from the Stewart train."

"Split off?" James repeated.

"Sure, split off." Mr. Grant eyed James and his pa carefully. "You had some folks head down to California by the Hudspeth Cutoff, did you not?"

"How did you know that?" James asked, astonished.

"How did I know that?" Mr. Grant hooted, clapping his hands and rubbing them. "Why, all the news comes through my trading post. Don't it, fellows?" he shouted at the men in the back.

Grunts of agreement rose from the men.

"I heard a Mr. Malcomb came to an untimely end," said Mr. Grant.

"Malcomb?" Pa asked. "You don't mean Meacham, by any chance?"

"Why sure, Meacham, that's what I said," Mr. Grant replied. "He left by the Hudspeth Cutoff, just him and his wife. But only she made it to the main California Trail. 'Pears her husband got bit by a snake. His leg all swole up, turned blue, and then he died." Mr. Grant slapped his thigh. "She didn't have the means to bury him even. I heard the story from a trader come up this way from Sacramento. The others from the Stewart train made it safe. They're at Sutter's Fort now."

James was speechless. Mean old Mr. Meacham, who'd planned on putting Bolt down and then tried to steal him back, dead of snakebite. His body left unburied for the buzzards and coyotes to fight over.

As much as he knew it was un-Christian, James couldn't help feeling justice had been served.

SIXTEEN

TWO PROPOSALS

That night the men and women of the Stewart train threw a final hoedown. Within days the families would be heading in their own directions, to pursue their own destinies. Already Pa had been talking to surveyors and land agents about likely prospects for homesteading. But for now, the only thought on everyone's mind was celebrating the safe arrival.

Ma dug deep into a trunk on the bed of the wagon and brought out the family's Sunday best.

An hour later, freshly bathed for the first time in weeks, James stepped into his gray serge trousers and tucked in his shirtfront. Both were an inch or two too small, but the tight fit didn't bother him. It was another sign of how much he'd grown.

He ran his hand over the stiff white cotton on his chest. It was much smoother than the coarse weave of his everyday clothes. "Jeremy," he called. "Come help me button my collar."

Jeremy stepped from around the wagon.

James whistled long and low. In his black dressing jacket with the matching pants and spit-polished shoes, hair slicked back and face shaved of its usual patchy brown beard, Jeremy looked almost . . . *presentable*. James could nearly imagine what Missy saw in him.

"Let me do that." Jeremy took the collar from James and wrapped it around his neck.

"Careful!" James gasped. "You don't have to choke me."

When Jeremy was finished, James buttoned his shoes and threw on his twill jacket. Then the brothers went to find their parents and sister.

Pa was handsome in his old-fashioned frock coat and four-in-hand. With his beard clipped close and a shiny black top hat perched on his head, he looked the gentleman through and through.

Elizabeth wore a dainty blue gingham dress with three layers of lacy collars. Her hair was braided into pigtails, with two green satin ribbons tied to the ends. When Jeremy tried to pick her up and swing her around, she yelled out for him to stop. She didn't want to be mussed.

But it was Ma who, in James's eyes, had undergone the most amazing transformation. He was so accustomed to seeing her as she was on the trail—

dirty, dusty, and tired, chasing after a husband and three children, cooking, tending the animals, never a moment's rest. She'd been wearing the same two frayed dresses for five months.

Now she had on a long dress made of lovely red calico with violets and primroses embroidered onto it. A velveteen sash went around the waist, and the collar and wrists were of real Belgian lace. Layers and layers of crinoline petticoats filled out the skirt, which was edged with still more lace. At the top of her head, her hair was pulled into a fat bun held in place by a long black-lacquer needle.

Her eyes were bright and her color high, and only by her rough red farm woman's hands did James know she wasn't a fancy city lady.

Carrying dishes that Ma had prepared that afternoon, the Greggs made their way to where the hoedown was planned. It was near the field where the wagons were camped, in a clearing in a wood. The dancing had begun, and the Greggs could hear the music long before they arrived.

Tall pines and hemlocks rose all around, filling the air with their pleasant odor. The stars caught the light from the moon low on the eastern horizon and flashed it back down.

Several large stumps were being used as tables for the food, which James examined with some interest. After eating nothing but snow, hardtack, and johnnycake in the mountains, he was eager for a feast. And it seemed the others in the party were too.

There was rabbit stew and buffalo jerky, left over from the journey. But there was also cured ham, fresh salmon and trout, a roast lamb, even fresh cow's milk, all purchased in Oregon City. Add to that the many pies stuffed with pears, apples, plums, and peaches from Fort Vancouver, and James was convinced there was no better place on earth than Oregon. Only the baskets filled with red raspberries made him doubt his judgment.

After an extended linger at the food tables, James wandered among the people. Ma had told him that Cady and her father wouldn't be here tonight—they had to nurse Mrs. Walker. James had mixed feelings about Cady's absence. On the one hand, she was his best friend. On the other, this party was just the sort of occasion that might give her ideas about kissing him again.

He only hoped her ma wasn't too seriously ill.

James momentarily spotted Sara standing by herself at the other side of the clearing. Between them folks danced and hopped, spun and waved their arms in the air to the bouncy rhythm of the fiddles.

He craned his neck to catch a better glimpse of Sara. She was wearing a deep-blue dress with a tight-fitting bodice. He decided to mosey on over to her.

"Howdy, Sara," he greeted her. He went to tip his hat, then realized he wasn't wearing one. He ran his fingers through his long brown hair. "Er, howdy," he repeated.

Sara stifled a giggle. "How do you do, Jamie?"

"All right, I reckon." He moved beside her, to face the center of the clearing. He glanced at her. He was as tall as she was, he noted. Maybe even taller.

"Lovely night, isn't it?" she said.

"Lovely," he agreed, staring out of the corner of his eye at her. "You certainly are. I mean, it certainly is."

Sara laughed. "Oh, James, you are a dear. You always cheer me up, you know that?"

"I'm glad." James meant it with all his heart. He hated to think of Sara as unhappy for even a minute. "By the bye, where's Will?"

Sara tilted her head back and forth. "He went off with Al and your brother."

James knew that even Lord Callanbridge had caught gold fever. "Jawing on their usual subject, are they?" he asked.

Sara smiled weakly. James took that as a yes.

Just then the music stopped, and the dancers broke up. Colonel Stewart strode to the middle of the clearing and raised his hands for quiet.

"Friends," he said. "I've led three other trains to the Oregon Territory, and none has been half as successful—free of strife and tragedy—as this one. I want to thank all of you for your stalwart perseverance and long-suffering patience through trying

141

times and imperfect leadership."

The crowd raised a great shout of approval, and then someone hollered, "Three cheers for Colonel Tom Stewart, the best train boss in the West!"

Three cheers went up, and then someone else yelled, "Three cheers for Pierre Delaroux, the finest guide ever to put on buckskins!"

Three more cheers rose up. James caught sight of Pierre Delaroux. It looked as if the big French trapper was blushing! And next to him the widow Loughery blushed just as fiercely.

Pierre Delaroux now stepped forward, into the center of the clearing. "My good friends," he said. "A joyous announcement I have to make tonight."

The crowd hushed. What kind of news could Mr. Delaroux possibly have?

"For many years I have lived the life of the trapper," Delaroux said. "Alone in the wood with only my gun and my own thoughts for companionship. Always I say, is the life for a man like me." Delaroux raised his forefinger dramatically. "But that now is changed, gone forever, poof!" He shrugged, held up his hands, and walked out of the circle.

The crowd buzzed in confusion. "What was that all about?" James whispered to Sara.

"I'm not sure, but I can guess," she said.

"What Pierre is trying to say, after his own fashion," the widow Loughery piped up, "is that he's asked me to marry him. And I've accepted his proposal."

142

A cheer went up that made the previous ones seem like the peeps of a newborn mouse. The women rushed to the widow, and the men crowded around Pierre Delaroux, slapping him on the back and tousling his hair.

James recalled the first day he'd met Mr. Delaroux. He'd seemed so forbidding then. James never thought he'd see him laugh while his hair got tousled by Jeremy, of all people.

While he stood with Sara and watched the festivities, James sensed that she wasn't sharing fully in the happiness. She was smiling, but it seemed like an empty smile.

"What's the matter, Sara?" James asked. "And don't say nothing, because I know something's troubling you."

"Oh, Jamie, I was thinking about the day Will proposed to me." She turned to him. "I do believe it was the happiest day of my life. No. No, I take that back. Our wedding day. *That* was the happiest day of my life."

James remembered. The ceremony was held on the banks of the North Platte.

"You remember the beautiful sunset that day?" Sara asked. "How brilliant red it was, like someone had thrown paint all over the sky?"

He nodded. Everyone had remarked on it.

"Little did we know what the beauty foretold," she said bitingly. "A dust cloud rising in the west, a storm that nearly buried us under. That's the way I feel about me and Will sometimes, Jamie. Like all that beauty in the beginning was only a sign of the pain to come."

James felt stabbed to the very core. His own dear Sara—for that was how he'd come to feel about her—regretting her marriage! Suffering these long weeks with nary a complaint. And now Will planning to run off to California.

James knew Will wasn't hurting her on purpose. Will was an honorable man. He was James's friend, almost like a brother to him, in some ways *more* of a brother than Jeremy had ever been. And yet . . . Something rose within James, and he knew he couldn't let Sara go on hurting. He had to do something.

James fell to his knees. "Sara, marry me," he blurted, taking her hand and pressing it to his forehead. It didn't matter who saw him or what they thought. "I don't care about Will. He's no good for you. I can't see you suffer any longer."

Sara pulled her hand away. Without a word, she turned and hobbled off quickly into the dark, dark wood.

James rose and followed her a few yards. "Sara . . ." he called, but she didn't stop.

He bowed his head and hid his face in his hands. What had he done?

SEVENTEEN

THE NEW BROTHER

A long while later, James returned to the party. The people were still dancing and singing, but he could share in none of it. He'd made an utter fool of himself, and more than that, he'd done nothing to help Sara. He'd only made her more unhappy.

James wandered through the laughing, shouting crowd, feeling more alone than he'd ever felt in his whole life. He was supposed to be glad to be in Oregon, but at this moment he wanted nothing more than to be back home in Franklin. He wished he'd never met Sara, or Will, or Cady, or any of them.

Out of the swirling mass of people his ma appeared in her red calico dress. "Jamie, you heard," she said.

James blinked. "Heard what?"

"About Mrs. Walker," Ma said. "You look terribly upset."

"Naw, just got some dust in my eyes." He brushed at his face. "What's this about Mrs. Walker?"

"She went into labor this afternoon," Ma said. "The journey down the Columbia must have been too much for her. I went back to check on her just a few minutes ago. She isn't well. Mr. Walker sent for the doctor in town. There's not much we can do but pray."

"How's Cady?" James asked.

Ma pursed her lips. "Jamie, I can't ask you to leave this party. I know you're having a time. But that little girl's mother might be dying. She needs you with her."

He nodded.

"Thank you, Jamie." Ma kissed his forehead, and James realized she had to stand on tiptoe to do it. "You're a good boy. And a fine man."

James ran down the trail that led through the wood, from the clearing to the field where the wagons were camped. The air was frostier now than it had been, and James's lungs burned deliciously. He found Cady sitting on a pail outside her family's tent.

"Howdy," James said, panting.

"Why, if it isn't President James K. Polk himself," she said dryly. "Those fancy duds are blinding me."

James sat on the ground next to her. "Likewise, I'm sure," he said, tweaking the ears of her panther-skin cape. "How's your ma faring?" he asked, serious now.

Cady lifted her shoulders. "Doc's in with her now. She's been laid up since before dinner."

"I'm sorry to hear that," James said.

Just then a small gasp came from the wagon behind them. They turned and saw Mr. Walker part the canvas flap and climb down.

"What is it, Father?" Cady asked.

"Nothing, darling, nothing." Mr. Walker hunkered next to his daughter and James. His hair was standing up at all angles on his head, and his eyes looked hollow. "Your mother's having a difficult time, is all."

Cady took a deep breath. "How difficult?"

"It's hard to say." He placed his hand on her shoulder. "The doctor's holding out hope. But it doesn't look good, for her or the baby."

"I see," Cady murmured.

"Cady," Mr. Walker said, "I'd like for you and James to take a little walk now. Why don't you go to the hoedown and have something to eat? You hardly had any dinner."

James took Cady's hand and stood. "I'll see that she's taken care of, Mr. Walker."

"Thank you, James." Mr. Walker rose and climbed back into the wagon. As he did, Mrs. Walker let out another small cry.

"Let's go, Cady," James said. "They don't need us hanging around here." He pulled her to her feet and led her away.

Instead of heading back to the clearing, however, James crossed the campsite to his own family's wagon. The remains of a small fire still smoldered, and James stoked it with new kindling and logs.

Soon a warm fire crackled, and he and Cady sat in front of it, beneath a buffalo-skin blanket. They could hear faint sounds of the hoedown in the distance.

"First Scott, and now Mother," Cady said quietly.

"You don't know she's going to . . ." James couldn't say it. "You know."

"You heard what Father said," Cady replied. "There's no use in my fooling myself."

James had no reassuring words for her. "It's been a long day," he said. "We should sleep now."

Cady drew the blanket to her neck and curled up against him. He glanced down at her. She looked ridiculous, wearing her panther cape under the buffalo skin. Yet endearing, in her own way.

After a few minutes her breathing slowed, became regular. He was sure she was asleep. He bent down and kissed her temple. "Good night, Cady," he whispered.

She smiled. "Good night, James."

In the morning Mr. Walker came for Cady. Mrs. Walker was still in labor. The doctor had returned to Oregon City. He could do nothing for her, he said. Now the widow Loughery was nursing her.

Pa had risen at sunup to ride out to a patch of

148

land some miles south, near the Molalla River. He'd heard the area was good rolling farmland, perfect for raising dairy cows, pigs, and goats, as well as barley, wheat, and just about any other crop you could name.

Back in his everyday clothes, James moped around the wagon. Whenever he thought about what he'd said to Sara the night before, his face burned with shame. She probably hated him now. And if she didn't hate him, she must think he was the silliest child she'd ever met.

Asking her to marry him! How could he have been so stupid? He was only twelve, and she was at least seventeen. A grown-up lady like her would have to laugh at a proposal from him.

He was worried about Mrs. Walker, too. What would happen to Cady if her mother died? Would she and her father be able to run a hardware store and a household on the frontier by themselves? He hated to think of what they might be forced to do—turn around and head back east.

James busied himself by feeding and watering Bolt, then brushing and combing him. He tossed a stick to Scraps for a while. Finally he went back to the wagon, propped himself against a wheel, and just sat in the dirt.

"James?" someone on the other side of the wagon said quietly.

He closed his eyes. It was Sara. The last person in

the world he wanted to talk to right now.

"James, are you angry at me?" she said, lowering herself stiffly onto the ground beside him.

"No, I'm not." James opened his eyes and stared straight ahead. He was too humiliated to look at her.

"Because I'd understand it if you were," she said. "I behaved terribly last night, running off like that. I owe you an apology. Can you ever forgive me?"

"There's nothing to forgive," he insisted. "I was a darn fool, and you were right to run off. You didn't want to let me see you laughing."

"Oh, Jamie, is that what you think?" Sara took his hand with both of hers and kneaded it between them. "That I was laughing at you? Jamie, believe me, no girl would laugh at so gallantly offered a proposal. I was simply . . . I don't know, confused. Distraught. Then you took me by surprise."

"It did sort of come out of nowhere, didn't it?" James asked.

"Well, not out of nowhere, no," she said. "You and I have a good understanding of each other. But I wasn't expecting a proposal, I'll admit that."

James smiled a little.

"You do forgive me, don't you?" she asked.

He was afraid his voice would crack if he tried to speak. He squeezed her hand in assent.

"Thank you," Sara whispered. They sat holding hands for a long, peaceful while.

"Oh, Jamie, I must tell you what happened last

night," Sara said brightly. "Will saw me running through the woods—"

James dropped his head onto his chest.

"Don't worry, James, Will didn't see you," she assured him. "Least he didn't say he did. Anyway, he came after me, and we had it out. I told him I thought he didn't love me anymore—that he wanted to run off to California to get away from me. And he said the only reason he wanted to strike it rich was so he could smother me in luxuries. Jamie, I realized what you'd been trying to tell me all along was right—Will does love me. There was a long time, after the accident, when I thought I was nothing but an ugly cripple. Yet Will never stopped loving me. I see that now. And I never stopped loving him with all my heart."

James looked over at her for the first time.

"I came looking for you afterward, Jamie," she said. "Please believe me. I knew how upset you must have been, but I couldn't find you anywhere. I didn't learn till this morning that you were comforting Cady.

"James," she said seriously, "I don't know if Will and I would ever have straightened ourselves out if it weren't for you. You saved our marriage, and I'll always be grateful to you for that. And I'll always treasure the memory of what you did last night."

"Aw, Sara." Shyly James drew his hand away from hers. "It was nothing."

"Nothing!" Sara laughed. "Only the most romantic proposal I ever received—and don't you tell Will I said that."

Suddenly James blanched. "You didn't tell Will about—"

"Of course I didn't," she said. She leaned over and kissed him on the cheek. "It's our secret."

James blushed to the roots of his hair as Sara got up and walked away. He was glad she and Will had put an end to their misunderstanding, and he was glad he'd played a part in bringing them back together. Even if it had been completely humiliating to him at the time. Sara was happy, that was the important thing. And James didn't even feel like a fool anymore for asking her to marry him.

"Jamie," his ma called, coming toward him from across the campground. With her was Elizabeth, who appeared to be crying.

"What is it, Ma?" James said, walking to meet them. "Why's Elizabeth crying?"

"Oh, the poor thing's frightened." Ma stooped to lift her daughter into her arms. "There, there, sweetness. I know it's upsetting."

"What's upsetting?" James asked.

"Jamie, Mrs. Walker passed away," Ma said. "Mrs. Loughery was with her when she breathed her last. Elizabeth and I had just gone over for a visit when we heard the sad news." She cuddled Elizabeth. "There, there, baby. It's sad, I know."

James had never had much affection for Mrs. Walker, but he knew how Elizabeth felt. Any death was grievous. He swallowed hard. "Poor Cady, with just her pa now."

"Oh, Jamie, I'm sorry," Ma said. "I didn't tell you. The baby lived. Mrs. Walker gave birth to a little boy this morning. He's small—no bigger than a kitten—and all red and wrinkly. Mrs. Loughery told me he was cold as a stone at first. Mrs. Walker put him to her breast and fed him—put the breath of life right into him. An hour later she herself had passed away." Ma clucked sorrowfully. "But the baby's healthy now, and Mrs. Loughery expects he'll survive."

A new baby, alive and healthy, and Mrs. Walker gone! James could scarcely believe it. "Does Cady know?" he asked.

"She was called in after the baby was born," Ma said. "After he was finished nursing, she took him from her mother. She was holding him when her mother died."

"I should go on over there," James said, half to himself.

"That would be a fine idea."

He started to walk off, then paused. "Ma—what's the baby's name?"

Ma frowned. "Why, Jamie, I plumb forgot to ask."

At the Walkers' wagon, James found Mr. Walker and the widow Loughery, along with Pierre

Delaroux and the colonel. They were discussing funeral arrangements.

"There's a preacher in town," Colonel Stewart said. "I know your wife would want a man of the cloth to preside."

"Rebecca was a religious woman," Mr. Walker allowed. "But I'm confident she would approve of your handling the ceremonies. That is, if you're willing."

"I'd be honored," said the colonel.

James wandered over to where Cady sat, in her arms the tiny infant wrapped in rabbit fur.

"He's real handsome," James observed politely of the puckered face.

Cady lifted her eyes and smiled. "He is, isn't he?"

"I'm sorry about your mother, Cady," James said. "If there's any way I or my family can help out . . ."

"We're all right," Cady said quietly, so as not to disturb the baby. "Hand me that pan, will you?" She gestured with her eyes.

James picked up the pan. In it was a puddle of white liquid. He held it out to Cady, and she dipped a corner of a small white rag into the liquid.

"Goat's milk and sugar," she said, placing the wet rag to the baby's lips.

James watched the baby gum the rag for a while. "You're good with him."

"Thanks," she said. "I better be. It's I who's going to be his mother now."

"What do you mean?" James asked. She couldn't

be the baby's mother. She wasn't even twelve yet.

"James, Mother's gone." She looked up at him again. "Father's going to be busy starting up a store. We can't afford to hire a nurse or a servant. Who else is going to be the mother?"

"But Cady, you're not old enough to—"

"James," she said sharply. "I am old enough. I'm old enough to rear this child, and I'm old enough to take care of Father, too. I'll do the cooking and cleaning, mending and fixing. I'll run the household, and I'll pitch in at the store, too, if I have to. Scott's gone, Mother's gone. There's no one else but me to do it." She was trying to sound proud and brave, but James heard the bleakness in her voice. "I'm the lady of the house now."

The baby started crying, and Cady stood up, patting his back gently. "There, there, precious. Mama's here. Everything's going to be all right," she murmured. "Everything's going to be all right."

EIGHTEEN

THE NEW SISTER

J ames was back at his family's wagon. It was almost dinnertime. Pa and Jeremy were feeding the animals. Elizabeth was wrestling with Scraps underneath the wagon. Ma was frying up corn cakes and salt pork. It was almost like they were on the trail again.

James had told his parents about Cady's having to be mother to the new baby. They hadn't seemed as shocked by the idea as he was. But they did seem unhappy about it.

After dinner the family gathered around the fire. Ma read aloud some of her favorite passages from Paul's Epistles. James listened to them respectfully. But truth be known, they didn't have enough action. As far as the Bible went, give him Joshua at the walls of Jericho any day.

Pa and Jeremy were opposites this night. While

Pa tinkered happily with the oxen's yokes, whistling to himself, Jeremy brooded silently. James knew his brother was moody sometimes, but tonight the black cloud hanging over his head was almost visible.

James was about to ask Jeremy what bee had got under his bonnet when Will stopped by. He greeted the family, then said, "James, can I speak to you a minute? In private?"

"Of course." As James walked away from the campfire, he wondered why Will needed to talk to him. He hoped Sara hadn't let slip the little matter of his proposal.

"I want to thank you," Will said.

James blew a sigh of relief. "What for?"

"For talking to Sara last night," he said. "I don't know what you said, but whatever it was, it convinced her to confront me. You tried to tell me plenty of times that Sara didn't hold anything against me, but I was too pigheaded to listen. Now I know how wrong I was. She never wanted anything from me but my love. I was a fool for thinking gold would make her happy."

"I tried to tell you that a hundred times," James said.

"Do you know," Will said, "she thought I wanted to go to California to get away from her?"

"I tried to tell you *that*, too," James said.

"And you were right about me being too hard on myself," Will went on. "I'm not perfect, and I never will be. Just like my daddy, I reckon. But that's no

158

reason for me to think I'm the dirtiest dog in town."

James was glad Will had come to his senses. "I suppose now you'll stay here in Oregon instead of gallivanting off to California," he said.

"Oh, no, what gave you that idea?" Will asked, perplexed. "We're still going to California. Now that Sara knows I'm not trying to be rid of her, she's more excited about California than I am. She's a spitfire, she is."

James stared at Will in wonderment.

"And not only that," Will said blithely, "Lord Callanbridge and your brother are coming with us."

"Jeremy?" James said, shocked.

"Why, sure. It was his idea in the first place. He suggested it all the way back at Fort Hall. You remember—you were there when he did."

"Yes, but . . . but . . . he can't go," James insisted. "He has to help Pa and me clear land, and build a house, and—"

"Jamie," Will said, "I don't want to take sides between you and your brother. But there's no stopping him if he's fixing on going."

James said good-bye to Will and returned to camp bristling. No wonder Jeremy had been skulking around all evening. He'd told his friends he was going to California, but he hadn't told his family. *He must be too ashamed to confess his plan*, James said to himself.

It was understandable that Lord Callanbridge

wanted to find gold, James thought. The lord was accustomed to being rich. And Will was from a big plantation with servants. It was only natural he'd want them out west. And Sara was from Boston, where everyone had fine silks and china.

But Jeremy was a farmer, like James. What did he need of gold? Farmers worked the soil and milked cows. Panning for gold might be all right for Lord Callanbridge, Will, and Sara, James decided—but not for Jeremy.

He walked over to where his brother sat staring into the fire. "I guess you need to get packing," he said bitterly.

"What are you talking about?" said Jeremy.

"If you're going to California, you have to get ready."

"What's all this about, Jamie?" Pa called. "What makes you say Jeremy's going to California?"

"Ask him." James pointed at his brother.

"I'm asking you," Pa said sternly. "Now answer the question."

"I just had a talk with Will," James said. "He told me that he and Sara are going to go down to California, and Jeremy's going with them."

"And you object to this plan?" Pa said.

"Why, of course I object!" James almost shouted. "Don't you?" Pa wasn't taking Jeremy's side, was he?

"What your brother does or doesn't plan to do," Pa said, "is none of your concern. You're not his father. If I have something to say to Jeremy, *I'll* say it."

"But—"

"No buts, Jamie," Pa said, mildly now. "When we left Missouri, Jeremy agreed to help us on the trail. He never promised to stay in Oregon once we got here." Pa turned to Jeremy. "It's not what I would choose, son, but you're a man now. You make your own decisions. If you want to go to California with Will and Sara, you have my blessing."

"Lord Callanbridge is going too," Jeremy said sheepishly. "He's sending to England for money to buy back his clothes, and to get prospecting supplies. It'll take a while for the money to get here, and Sara needs more time for her leg to heal. So we won't leave until spring. Till then I can help you get settled."

Pa nodded approvingly. "You've thought this through, I gee."

"Oh, Jeremy!" Bursting into tears, Ma ran over and grappled him around the neck. "My baby!"

"Ma, Ma!" Jeremy cried, laughing. "Didn't you hear what Pa just said? I'm a man now. I can't go around being sobbed over by my ma."

Ma held him at arms' length. "I don't care how old you are. Don't you ever say I can't sob over you." She shook him hard, then hugged his head. "You'll always be my little baby."

Even James was laughing now. It was going to take some getting used to, this idea that his brother was leaving. But Pa was right. Jeremy was a man now. He could make his own decisions.

Even if they were the wrong ones, James added silently.

The next morning the Greggs attended Mrs. Walker's funeral. Colonel Stewart spoke of the dead woman's loss of her own son, how it had made her stronger. Coming to a new, wild land, she'd hoped to make life better for her children. One had perished, as had she. And yet two remained, and a good father besides.

James stood with Cady, who held the baby. All through the ceremony, the baby sucked on a wet rag. He didn't cry once, though he was the only one among the mourners who didn't.

"In former days," the colonel said, "the angels dwelled with people on earth. In our fallen state, we must cross over to the country of death to see the angels. And now I ask you all to pray for Rebecca Walker's soul, which is now on its way across the great bridge to heaven."

Mrs. Walker was lowered into the ground and the dirt piled on top. No headstone was laid on her grave. Mr. Walker hoped to buy one, once his store was established and he had a little money.

Afterward the mourners drifted over to the Greggs' wagon, where James's ma had prepared some biscuits with molasses, a bit of ham, and some stewed apples.

162

Though the food smelled tempting, no one ate much. With this funeral, James felt, the trail really had come to an end. He lived in Oregon. This was his home. Soon his friends Will, Sara, and Lord Callanbridge would be leaving, along with Jeremy. James's family would move to the country while Cady stayed in town and cared for the baby.

James was going to be all alone.

"I reckon you're getting to be pretty fond of that baby," James said to Cady.

"Fond, yes," she said. "But he's a lot of work. He needs feeding constantly, and he cried half the night. And you know about changing babies."

Actually, James didn't know about changing babies, and he preferred to keep it that way.

"I miss my mother already, James," Cady said. "I know she was difficult, but she loved me. And I don't have any experience rearing children." Cady stroked the baby's fine blond hair. "It's already more work than I expected, and he's only a day old. I don't know how I'm going to be able to do everything that needs doing all by myself."

Just then James's ma walked up. "Cady, maybe you won't have to," she said.

"What do you mean?" Cady asked. "We can't afford a nurse."

"James's pa and I have been talking to your father," Ma said. "I was thinking, once we get settled, that I could use a young woman around the house

163

to help me with the chores. Elizabeth tries, but she's only six. I need an older girl."

"You want Cady to come live with us?" James asked, unable to believe what his ma was saying.

"If it agrees with her," Ma said. "And with you, of course."

"Why, that would be great!" James said. He wouldn't be all alone on the farm. Sure, Cady was a burr under his saddle every now and then, but on the whole he could put up with her.

"Now, hold on, James," Cady said. "Mrs. Gregg, who's going to care for Father? Who'll cook his meals, and mend his clothes? And what about Alonzo?"

"Why, your pa will take his meals at the hotel in town, dear," said James's ma. "And he can hire a seamstress when he needs one. It'll be hard at first, but once he has his store, he'll have money to spare."

Cady nodded thoughtfully.

James screwed up his face. "Who on earth is Alonzo?"

Ma looked quizzically at Cady. "Yes, who's Alonzo?"

"Why, *he* is." She held up the little baby. "Father said I could name him, so I did. Alonzo Walker. I always liked that name, Alonzo."

At least since the colonel told his story about Alonzo Tanner, the bravest man he ever met, James said to himself.

"Cady," Ma said, "little Alonzo will come with you, to stay with us. I'll help you with him. I've had

164

plenty of practice rearing boys." Her eyes crinkled merrily. "Maybe someday I'll get it right."

While Cady laughed, her father and James's pa ambled over.

"Have you discussed it with her?" Mr. Walker asked James's ma.

"She's considering," Ma said. She turned to Cady. "I sure could use another hand around the house."

"Cady, my darling," Mr. Walker said. "Would you like to live with the Greggs for a while? It'll only be till the baby—er, Alonzo—is out of diapers. By then I'll be set up in the store, and we'll be able to fend for ourselves."

"But Father, that'll be years," Cady said. "How can I go so long without ever seeing you?"

"You'll be able to see him more often than that," James's pa said. "We'll be settling only eight miles down the road, on the Molalla River. I saw the land yesterday—beautiful soil, a high ridge for the house to set on. Even a little trout stream on the property."

So that's what he was so pleased about last night, James thought.

"You can ride into town as often as you like," Pa said to Cady. "I'm sure James won't mind lending you Bolt."

"Really?" Cady asked. "James, you'd let me take Bolt some days?"

"If you let me wear your panther-skin cape, I might," he teased.

"Please come live with us, Cady," Ma said. "You're practically one of the family already."

Cady looked from face to face. "James, you just got yourself a new sister!"

And so it was decided. Cady and her new brother would join the Greggs on their farm outside Oregon City.

That night, as James lay in his tent at the campground, he thought about all he'd seen and done in the five months since he'd left Independence, Missouri.

Following the Oregon Trail had been a long, hard labor, and there was plenty more work to be done. Tomorrow he, Jeremy, and Pa were riding out to the new homestead, to clear trees on the ridge. Within a few days, they hoped to have built a rough road leading to a small cabin. Later a better road, and a bigger house, would be constructed.

It would be nice to have a real house to live in again, James thought. *A house is warm and safe. Unlike a tent, a house can't get trampled by a buffalo. You don't have to pick up and move your house every day.*

Yes, James thought, *it'll be nice not to be on the trail.*

But part of him already longed for the freedom of the road, where every day brought something new. Those were some of the best days of his life, and he wondered if they would ever come again.

He thought about his brother, and how Jeremy

wanted to move on to California. Maybe Jeremy felt some of the same longing for the trail as he did.

Maybe James could even join Jeremy, and travel down to California. And from there, who knew?

But it would never be the same. Never again would James and the other emigrants line the wagons in the traveling formation, nor hitch them together in the nightly circle.

In Oregon City there was land to clear and crops to plant, houses to raise and furniture to carve. There would be schools and churches, legislatures and jails. Never again would he and his family roast fat elk or buffalo over an open fire, or tell stories and sing songs beneath a limitless and utterly free sky.

A great adventure was coming to an end, an episode in James's life that, no matter how he longed for it, he could never repeat.

He'd made a pact with Cady and her brother Scott to return to Independence Rock in the year 1900. When Scott died, James swore to himself he'd keep the pact. Now he realized that, when the time came, he'd do it as much for himself as for his dead friend.

And yet he knew it would never be the same. Even if he returned to all the old places along the Oregon Trail, even if he did it by ox team and covered wagon, he wouldn't be able to recapture days gone by. Too many had died, too much had already faded into the past.

The land was changing daily, and James was part of the change. And he knew that he, too, was changing.

As James drifted slowly off to sleep, he consoled himself with the thought that the times he'd shared with Cady, Scott, his family, and the others were locked safely away forever in his heart.